Alberta Alibi

Alberta Alibi

Dayle Campbell Gaetz

ORCA BOOK PUBLISHERS

Other books in this mystery series
by Dayle Campbell Gaetz

Mystery from History
Barkerville Gold

National Library of Canada Cataloguing in Publication Data
Gaetz, Dayle, 1947-
Alberta alibi / Dayle Campbell Gaetz.

ISBN 1-55143-404-0

I. Title.

PS8563.A25317A64 2005   jC813'.54   C2005-904764-X

First published in the United States, 2005
Library of Congress Control Number: 2005931361

Summary: Sheila, Rusty and Katie race to save Sheila's father
in a fight with unscrupulous developers.

Orca Book Publishers gratefully acknowledges the support for its
publishing programs provided by the following agencies: the Government of
Canada through the Book Publishing Industry Development Program (BPIDP),
the Canada Council for the Arts, and the British Columbia Arts Council.

Cover design by Lynn O'Rourke
Cover illustration by Ljuba Levstek

Orca Book Publishers
PO Box 5626, Stn. B
Victoria, BC Canada
V8R 6S4

Orca Book Publishers
PO Box 468
Custer, WA USA
98240-0468

www.orcabook.com
Printed and bound in Canada
08 07 06 05 • 4 3 2 1

To Jupiter

Acknowledgments

I would like to thank Travel Alberta and the helpful folk who work there for providing so much useful information and answering all of my questions. I wish to thank, as well, all the hardworking people involved with the Nature Conservancy of Canada. Their ongoing efforts ensure that key areas of Canada's wildlife habitat will be preserved for generations to come. Special thanks, as always, to my editor, Andrew Wooldridge, for his invaluable suggestions and advice.

1

Almost there, almost there, almost there. The words bounced back and forth inside her skull, over and over, until she wanted to scream. Instead she turned the volume up another notch. Music surged through the earphones, crashed into her brain. But the words only got louder, keeping time to the music. *Almost there! Almost there! Almost there!*

Sheila couldn't stand it another second. She had to get out of here. But how do you escape from the backseat of a pickup truck that's roaring down an Alberta highway towing a trailer? Katie beside her, Rusty next to Katie, Katie's grandma in the front, GJ driving. Too many people! How could she possibly think?

She pressed her hands against the sides of her head. She felt like yanking those stupid yellow earphones off and tossing them on the floor. But if she did, everyone would stare at her and want to know what was wrong. From the corner of her eye she saw Katie put down her mystery novel and turn toward her with that curious tilt to her head that meant Katie knew something was up.

Sheila refused to look at her. She knew Katie's forehead would be wrinkled and her dark brown eyes narrowed in suspicion. If Katie started asking questions, it would be impossible to shut her up. Sheila forced herself to calm down. She took a deep breath and made her face look relaxed so she wouldn't need to talk. She could not talk right now, not to anyone, not even her best friend. Her head was jammed too full and she needed time to think.

Sheila turned down the volume, right down to nothing, and snapped her fingers as if she was keeping time to the music instead of those two words, *Almost there.* She turned away from Katie and looked out the small side window.

They weren't in British Columbia anymore. Actually, they hadn't been for a couple of days. Sheila had to admit that the restored gold-rush town at Barkerville, where they had been the week before, was way less boring than she expected. She could almost understand why Rusty was so into history. And she didn't even mind that Katie got them all involved in another of her *cases*. As long as she kept busy, Sheila didn't need to think about where they were headed next.

After Barkerville they drove through the Yellowhead Pass, turned south at Jasper and stopped at the Athabasca Glacier. They stayed overnight at a campground high in the mountains and rode out onto the Columbia Icefield in one of those bus things with great monster tires. That was fun.

Then they drove the parkway that wound south through all those amazing mountains to Banff. On the way they saw two black bears, a moose, loads of bighorn sheep and tons of wapiti.

This afternoon, after lunch and shopping in Calgary, they turned south onto Highway 2. That's when it hit her. Wham! Right in the face. They really were in Alberta. The Rocky Mountains, a giant wall of jagged rock capped with snow, loomed above the low, forested foothills to her right. On her other side, the foothills flattened into grassland that rolled on forever under a sky so blue it brought tears to her eyes.

That's when she clamped her earphones on and cranked up her CD player. No one could talk to her, but she couldn't stop herself from looking out the window. Everything looked familiar and different at the same time. How could that be? She tried not to look when they passed High River and turned west again, heading straight for those high peaks, rock gray against that pure blue sky.

But not for long. It seemed like no time before they reached Highway 22–"The Cowboy Trail" some people called it–and GJ swung the truck and trailer onto it. After that, time slowed down. Near the little town of Longview, Sheila saw a road sign ahead. It pointed to the Bar U Ranch, a National Historic Site. Her stomach fluttered.

Almost there.

Sheila hadn't set foot in Alberta since she was ten, just over two years ago, and she had missed the ranch every single day. She missed Silver too. But more than anything, she missed her dad. And that was the scariest part because Sheila knew her dad didn't miss her anywhere near as much as she missed him. If he did, he would have come to see her once in a while, as he had promised.

"You'll be less than two hours from Calgary by plane," he said just before she and Mom drove away from the ranch forever. "I'll see you every month."

Right. He had flown out to Victoria exactly three times. And the last time she saw him was last year, before Christmas. He didn't even want to see her on Christmas Day!

That's why her stomach was doing jumping jacks all over the place. It was so nice of Katie and Rusty's grandparents to drive her to the ranch so she could visit for a few days. But her dad hadn't exactly leapt up and down with joy when she talked to him on the phone. All he said was "When did you say you'd be here?"

"Dad, I already told you twice. July 21."

"Oh! Well, I guess you'll want your old room?"

You can't beat that for enthusiasm.

If Dad didn't want to be bothered with her, at least she'd be able to ride Silver. Maybe *he* would be happy to see her. The thought of her beautiful, golden horse brought a smile to Sheila's lips.

"What's funny?" Katie demanded.

Sheila turned back from the window. "Huh?"

"You were laughing. What's funny?" Katie spoke really loudly so Sheila would be able to hear over the nonexistent music.

"I'm not laughing, I'm smiling. I like this song." She snapped her fingers a few times for Katie's sake, then turned up the volume. She smiled again, partly because she really did like this song and partly because she had Katie and Rusty so totally fooled. They were convinced she listened to modern rock music. No one had guessed her terrible secret.

She was into country music. It was the only way Sheila knew of to feel close to her dad. Outside the window, everything started looking way too familiar, so she closed her eyes. She snapped her fingers, just in case someone was looking at her.

"Almost there!" GJ called out.

Oh no! The words had gone. Now they came rushing back. She opened her eyes. She wasn't ready. She didn't want to see him. Maybe they could just drive on by. Turn around and head for Saskatchewan. But there was the wooden sign, same as always, nailed to a fencepost at the end of their long, winding driveway. The Triple W Ranch. You'd think he would have crossed off the "Triple" by now and made it The Lone W Ranch. Her dad said the sign used to say "The Waltons," but everyone laughed when they saw it because of some old TV show or something.

"Is this it?" GJ asked, slowing down. He glanced over his shoulder.

Sheila was tempted to shake her head. No. Keep going. Don't stop. Please! Instead she nodded at GJ and stared down at her hands. The music wailed in her ears. She hated it. She switched it off and stared out the window. Her throat hurt.

Almost there.

2

There it was, same as ever, on top of a small rise, surrounded by cottonwood trees. A big, sprawling, two-story house with white wood siding and a covered, wraparound porch. Wide windows overlooked ripening hayfields.

Sheila's heart pounded against her ribs. Her mouth went dry. What would her father say? What would he do? Would he run out the door and give her a hug? Would he say he was sorry about forgetting her birthday last month? Would he tell her he was busy and ask if she could come back some other time?

They pulled into the flat, dusty farmyard. GJ swung the wheel and pulled truck and trailer to a stop beside the barn.

For the next minute no one moved. Sheila held her breath and listened to her heart beat-beat-beating.

"Sheila?" Katie tapped on the plastic earphone, loud against her ear. "Sheila, turn off the CD, we're here!"

Sheila bit her lip, took off the headphones. By then Gram had opened the passenger door and slid to the ground. She pulled open the narrow back door for Sheila. "Let's go find your dad!"

Hot dust filled her nostrils as she crossed the yard with Katie and Gram. Dust and manure and the familiar warm, dry smell of sun-baked fields. Two steps up to the wooden porch, five steps to the door. It still looked the same, this house she was born in. But different too, almost like the home of a stranger. It didn't seem quite as big as she remembered, and she hadn't noticed how badly the paint was worn from the wooden porch or how the boards creaked beneath her feet when she stepped on them. She reached the front door. Bright red. It was supposed to be green. She stopped and stared at it.

Should she knock or just walk in? She couldn't decide so she knocked and turned the doorknob at the same time. Except that the doorknob wouldn't turn. And no one came to the door. They were locked out.

Now what? This was the one thing that never once occurred to her. Sheila had known he might not greet her with open arms. He might not be as pleased to see her as she wanted him to be, but she never thought he would simply go away and lock the door.

They never locked the door when she lived here, not in the daytime.

"I expect he must have been called away by something that couldn't wait," Gram said, slipping an arm around Sheila's shoulders. "Let's go to the trailer and make ourselves some iced tea while we wait. I don't know about you, but I'm parched."

"Me too." Katie sounded artificially cheerful. "And let's have some of those cookies we bought at the bakery in Calgary."

Sheila nodded. She couldn't speak. They should never have come. Her father didn't want her here, that's why he took off. Either that or he forgot. She really didn't know which was worse.

They took folding chairs from the trailer and set them up in the shade of cottonwoods, where they settled to sip iced tea and munch cookies. Sheila didn't sip or munch. She sat quietly, staring into her glass, watching the ice cubes melt. She wanted to go home.

"I'm sure he'll be along soon," Gram said again.

GJ looked glum. He leaned forward in his chair, his forearms resting on his knees, and stared straight ahead at two sleek, black horses in the corral. Sheila had never seen them before. She wondered where Silver was, but couldn't summon the energy to go look for him.

Rusty polished off another cookie and put his head back, gazing up through leafy green foliage to patches of blue sky. A little beam of sunlight landed on the top of his head and lit up his red hair like fire. "I don't mind staying here for a few days," he said, "but you'll never catch me on a horse."

Katie occasionally glanced up from her book, a sad look in her dark brown eyes, then lost herself in the mystery story again.

"Someone's coming!" GJ said. He stood up and took a few steps toward the fields, his hands on his hips.

Sheila leapt out of her chair and darted to the corral fence. She stepped onto the bottom rail and rested her arms on the top one. "It's Silver!" she cried. A golden horse galloped toward them, closely followed by a cloud of dust. Sheila smiled. That's what happened. Silver must have been out to pasture and her dad had gone to get him for her, but he took longer than expected to find her horse and now, here he was.

As horse and rider drew closer, Sheila's smile sagged. The rider looked small, way too small to be her father, who was a tall, broad-shouldered man. Silver slowed to a trot and then a walk as he neared the fence; his long tail swished bright silver in the sunlight. The rider wore jeans, a white T-shirt and a black cowboy hat. He dismounted, opened a gate, led Silver through and started up the driveway toward them. Definitely too small to be her father, he was only a boy, no bigger than Rusty.

Sheila felt like running up to him, demanding to know who he was and why he was riding her horse. Why did he have her dad's hat? But she remained very still on the fence, eyes narrowed, watching.

Katie came up beside her. "Who's he?"

"How should I know!" Sheila snapped. She wished Katie would leave her alone. Why didn't they all just go away and leave her alone?

The minute he was led into the yard, Silver whinnied and pranced with excitement. He pulled on the reins, trying to get to Sheila. "Easy now." The boy held Silver back. He took off his hat and wiped his brow with the back of his hand. He had a tanned, square face, straight brown hair and gray eyes that looked wary. He glowered at the five of them. "Who are you?" he demanded.

"Who are *you*?" Katie ran toward him. "And what are you doing with my friend's horse?"

The boy looked from Katie to Sheila, frowning. Then his mouth and eyes got round at the same time. "Are you Sheila? Wow! Chris was right, you do have a million freckles. So how come you're here today?"

Even if Sheila was ready to answer, she didn't have a chance with Katie on the job. "She said she'd be here on the twenty-first, didn't she? And today's the twenty-first. So who are you anyway?"

"Chris said you were coming tomorrow," the boy said.

Chris. Her dad, Chris Walton. Who was this kid? Before Sheila could ask, there was a screech of tires on the paved road. Seconds later an old beat-up truck came bumping and rattling up the driveway, almost lost in billowing dust. It skidded to a halt near the trailer. The driver's door flew open and out burst her dad.

"Sheila!" he called. He whipped off his black cowboy hat; his light brown hair flew in the air and settled over his forehead as he ran toward her. "I lost track of the date! Didn't realize it was the twenty-first till I got to town and went to the bank. I'm sorry! I wanted to be here when you arrived." He had reached the fence by then and flung his arms open to give her a hug.

Sheila clung to the top rail and shied away from him. She looked at the boy. "Who is he and what is he doing with my horse?"

Her father's arms fell to his sides. "I guess I should

have told you sooner," he began, "but I didn't know how to get started. I decided it might be best if you could meet him in person."

She waited.

"This is Huntley James. Remember the Arnesens?"

Sheila nodded. The Arnesens were a really nice elderly couple who owned a neighboring ranch. "So?"

"So Mr. Arnesen died quite suddenly last year and their daughter, Adele, came home from Toronto to help her mother. But just recently Mrs. Arnesen had to go into a nursing home, and Adele is, uh, dealing with the ranch. I knew Adele from school, we're old friends."

"So?" Sheila asked again. Why was he telling her all this stuff? What did it have to do with this, what's his name, this Hartley? She glared at the boy, who still clung to Silver's reins.

"Huntley is Adele's son and he's...that is, she's..."

"What!?!"

"Huntley's staying with me while Adele's away."

"I see. So you're *baby*sitting him."

"You could say that, yeah."

"I'm helping out on the ranch," Huntley said firmly. Then he went on talking as if no one else was there. "Chris, did you hear about the night watchman over at the development?"

"No, what about him?"

"Someone shot him last night. He's in hospital at High River. Police are looking for someone who drives an old blue pickup."

All eyes flicked over to the pickup truck parked next to the trailer. It gave off a metallic ticking sound as it cooled, and a puff of steam escaped from its grill while dust settled quietly over its pale blue paint.

3

Oh no! Not again! Not another mystery! Sheila glanced at Katie and knew her friend was itching to ask some questions. But Katie's grandparents were watching closely now, and Sheila saw Katie swallow her excitement. Sheila knew her friend must be practically biting her tongue to keep from asking, *What development? What night watchman? Why would someone shoot at him? And why are they looking for an old blue truck?*

Sheila's dad laughed. "An old blue pickup? They'll have to visit half the ranches from High River to Fort Macleod if that's the only clue they've got."

Huntley laughed too. "That's what I told Wendell. He saw the truck."

Katie made an odd sound in her throat. It started like "Wh-oo" and ended in a cough. Of course Katie wanted to know who Wendell was, but Sheila didn't much care as she watched the boy disappear into the barn leading Silver. She followed.

Her dad's voice stopped her. "Sheila, aren't you going to introduce me to your friends?"

"Uh, yeah, I guess so." She hated introducing people; it always felt so awkward, and all she really wanted to do right now was go talk to her horse. That and boot the little brat Hartley out of the barn so she could groom Silver herself. But Gram and GJ had been so nice to her, she didn't want them to think she was rude.

She took a deep breath. "Okay. Gram, GJ, this is my dad, Chris Walton. And, Dad, this is my best friend, Katie Reid and her cousin, Rusty Gates. He's my friend too," she added as an afterthought. Rusty looked surprised and then he grinned at her.

"We're so happy to meet you," Gram said, shaking Sheila's dad's hand. "I'm Lynne Sampson and this is my husband, Jerry. The kids call him GJ, short for Grampa Jerry."

While the adults settled in to talk about boring stuff, Katie wandered over to inspect the pickup truck. Sheila was glad Katie didn't have her notebook in hand because for sure she'd start taking notes, and Dad would want to know why.

Looking bored, Rusty sat back down on his folding chair. He picked up a cookie and the book Gram bought him in Calgary. Something about early settlement in the foothills.

"I'm going to see Silver," Sheila announced and stomped into the barn.

The mingled smells of hay and horse and old leather made her suddenly feel at home. The light was dim and her eyes took a moment to adjust. Then she saw Silver at the far end of the barn, dark and shadowy in the weak light. He was haltered and tied to a post to keep him still while that brat of a boy removed his saddle.

"I want to groom him!" Sheila shouted, knowing she sounded rude, but for once she didn't care.

The brat turned around, holding the saddle in his arms. He grinned. "I figured you would."

Silver whinnied softly and Sheila forgot all about the boy as she walked up to her horse and stroked his soft muzzle. "Silver, I've missed you so much!" she whispered. She pulled out a carrot from her pocket, one she had brought all the way from home. It was limp and rubbery, but Silver didn't seem to mind.

"I bet you want to know why I'm really here," the brat said.

"I don't care, Harley. Just so long as you leave me and my horse alone."

He stood there, waiting.

Sheila tried to ignore him, hoping he would go away. She ran her fingers through Silver's thick silver mane and whispered softly to him, but the boy didn't go away and finally she couldn't stand it any longer. "What?" she half turned, far enough that she could see his shoulder but not his face.

"My name's not Harley, it's Huntley, and I think you do want to know. You're just too stubborn to ask."

"I'm not stubborn!" she yelled so loudly Silver shied away from her. "Sorry, boy," she whispered. Then, "All right, tell me, if it will make you go away."

"Your dad is my mom's boyfriend."

The shock of his words shot right through her. They brought instant tears to her eyes. Sheila blinked and buried her face in Silver's neck. "Go away, Harley."

"I won't go unless you call me Huntley."

"Harley, Huntley, Humphrey, who cares? They're all stupid names if you ask me!"

She heard his footsteps retreating through the barn and guessed she had hurt his feelings. But she didn't care. He deserved it. How dare he tell lies about her dad? Deep down, her dad still loved her mom, Sheila knew that. They would all live together again, here on the Triple W Ranch. It was only a matter of time.

Sheila was still brushing Silver when she heard a soft footstep behind her. "Can't you just leave me alone?" she snapped.

"Sheila?"

It was Gram's voice. Sheila whirled around. "Oh, sorry. I thought you were that boy."

"Huntley? He seems like a nice boy. Wasn't it thoughtful of him to walk all that way out and bring your horse in for you?"

Sheila said nothing. She felt like crying.

"Are you all right, Sheila?"

She nodded, smiled. "I'm good," she sniffed.

"Sometimes it's hard to come back and see changes."

When Sheila didn't answer, Gram continued, "GJ and I are just about ready to head out to meet our friends from High River. But if you'd like, we can stay until tomorrow." She glanced at her watch. "If I phone now, I can catch them before they leave for the cabin we've rented in Kananaskis Country."

Sheila shook her head. "I'm fine. I'm just excited to see Silver again."

"Are you sure? Because once we're in the mountains you won't be able to reach us by phone, so if—"

"Hey! That's what I like to see, girl and horse reunited!" GJ stepped up behind Gram and slipped an arm around her shoulders. "Are we ready to roll?"

Gram nodded. She gave Sheila a quick hug. "You'll be fine," she said. "We'll see you in a few days. Have a great time!"

Sheila nodded and watched the two of them walk from the barn. A solid, broad-shouldered man and a tall slender woman, they were dark silhouettes against the bright light of the open barn door.

Outside, she heard voices, the slam of a truck door, the roar of a diesel engine and the rumble of tires rolling down the driveway. She held on tight to Silver to keep from running after them.

If it weren't for Katie and Rusty, Sheila would have put that saddle right back on Silver and taken off into the green hills that lay at the foot of the mountains. She wouldn't have come back until dark. But she was the one who had invited her friends to stay here with her while their grandparents took a well-deserved break. She couldn't very well desert them as soon as they arrived, when neither of them wanted to be here in the first place. Katie wasn't much interested in ranch life, or in cattle or horses for that matter. All she seemed to care about these days was being the Great Detective.

As for Rusty, Sheila suspected he was scared to go near horses or cattle, even though he would never admit it. For sure, Rusty had proved he could be brave when necessary but, even so, he was the most nervous kid she had ever met. Of course, he had good reason to be; he was also the most accident-prone kid she had met in her life.

If she took off now, they would be stuck alone with Dad and that horrible boy. So she led Silver into his stall, checked his food and water and walked slowly from the barn.

4

She should have known Katie would be taking notes. Seated on a folding chair, curled over her notebook, Katie turned her head to study the old blue truck. She tapped her pen against her forehead, then scribbled like crazy again.

Sheila ran over. "Where is everyone?" she demanded. Her voice came out loud and angry, surprising her. Sheila didn't feel anything like her normal self today. Instead of the quiet, thoughtful girl most people thought she was, today Sheila felt like yelling at everyone. There must be something in the Alberta air— maybe it was the high altitude that made her feel this way. Or maybe it was her dad or that boy, or maybe it was Katie.

Katie looked up, startled. "Uh, your dad asked the boys to help him carry the groceries. They're going to make hamburgers and hot dogs for dinner. I'm starved, aren't you?"

"Hmm." Sheila plunked herself down on a chair near her friend. She leaned back, stretched out her legs and stared at the toes of her white running shoes. "What are you writing about?"

Katie kept scribbling, ignoring her.

"Katie, I asked what you're writing about."

"Nothing. I'm just making notes about the truck, you know, and the mud stuck up in the wheel wells? I took a sample." She waved a little plastic bag. It was from the package Katie had purchased in Calgary, and it had a little clot of black mud in the bottom corner. "And," she picked up another bag, "this was stuck in the front bumper, so I collected it too." The bag contained a twig with flat green leaves attached.

"What for?"

"So we can prove where the truck has been in case, you know, the police come by. So we can prove he's innocent."

"Of course he's innocent! Do you think my dad goes around shooting people?"

"No, Sheila, I just think...nothing."

Katie returned to her notes. She glanced at Sheila and quickly looked away. Sheila couldn't help but notice the bright pink patches on Katie's cheeks and the way her dark eyes danced in all directions but never landed directly on Sheila's face.

Katie started to close her notebook. Without stopping to think, Sheila burst out of her chair, dived at Katie, snatched the notebook from her hands and ran.

"Give that back! No one reads my notebook!"

Sheila kept her finger in the book to mark the page, tucked it under her arm and took off around the barn. From there she ran as fast as she could across the field. She could easily outrun Katie, she knew that. Sheila was the fastest runner in their school. Maybe the fastest in Victoria if getting all those first-place ribbons in the previous month's track meet meant anything. She ran to the far end of the field and stopped at the fence. A quick glance over her shoulder told her she had just enough time. Katie was barreling toward her like an angry bull.

She flipped open the notebook and read quickly.

July 21

Examined truck. It's an old, blue pickup all right, with loads of rust.

Found mud, still damp, stuck up behind the fenders above the back wheels. Where did that come from? Is there black mud between here and town on a dusty, hot day like today?

Also found a piece of tree caught in front bumper. Think it's aspen, need to check tree book. How did it get there?

Truck doors locked. Gun rack across back window. No gun.

There were more scribblings, but Katie arrived then and snatched the book away. "What do you think you're doing?" she screeched. "That's *my* book, you have no right to take it!"

Katie looked spitting mad, but Sheila was angry too. Deep down, sizzling angry. "What are you trying to do? Send my dad to prison?" she yelled.

"No, Sheila, I want to help!"

"Then you'd better mind your own business from now on." Sheila stomped back toward the barn. This was the worst day of her life. No, it wasn't. It was the second worst. The worst was two years ago.

She should never have come back here, and for sure she shouldn't have brought Katie. That girl always meddled in everyone else's business, and right now Sheila had no idea why she had ever thought of Katie as her best friend. Well, not anymore. She was tired of Katie's nosiness and tired of trying to keep Katie out of trouble.

Sheila had to get out of here. She would march

right into the barn, saddle Silver and take off into the hills. No telling when she might come back. Maybe she would ride all the way home to Victoria. Wouldn't that surprise them all?

She stormed around the corner of the barn.

And stopped in her tracks. Katie came up beside her. They both stared at the white SUV parked next to the blue pickup truck. It had a yellow, red and blue stripe along its side, a crest on the door and a small blue silhouette of a horse and rider on the back fender. Across its roof was a row of lights. The RCMP.

"They must be in the house," Katie whispered.

Sheila thought that was fairly obvious, since no one was in sight, but she didn't say a word. She only stared at the SUV and thought about her mom. Police cars often stopped in front of their little house in Victoria. On-duty officers sometimes came by for coffee when her mom wasn't working, because they were friends.

Mom was a police officer too. Dad wasn't. And Sheila had a feeling the Mounties were not here for a cup of coffee and a home-baked muffin.

"I wonder if they have searched the truck yet," Katie mused.

"Not without a search warrant," Sheila informed

her. She thought that was right, that police needed a search warrant before they could touch private property, but she wasn't sure. She wished Mom were here so she could ask her.

"If they do, they'll find the mud and the rest of that tree branch. I just broke a piece off, I didn't take it all."

"So?"

"So nothing. I'm just saying..."

"Let's go see what's happening."

"Okay." Katie walked over to the chair, tucked the two plastic bags inside her notebook and picked up her pen from the ground. She carried everything with her toward the door.

Sheila didn't object. She had to admit that Katie was pretty good at figuring things out. After all, she had solved the mystery at the old house in Victoria and figured out where the gold was hidden at Barkerville. Of course, Katie couldn't have done it without her help, and Rusty's too, but if her dad was in trouble, maybe it was a good thing to have Katie on the job. Unless he was guilty...but she wouldn't even think about that.

The two girls walked side by side toward the house. "Just don't annoy them by asking questions, okay?"

"Of course not."

"I mean it!" Sheila whispered fiercely as they stepped onto the front porch.

"You know me," Katie replied.

"That's the problem."

Sheila tried not to look at the ugly red door as she pushed it open. And she tried not to worry about what Katie might do next.

Inside was a square entrance hall with a dark plank floor worn to a wide groove down the center by the passing of many feet. On the wall to the right of the door, a row of wooden pegs stood empty except for a couple of black cowboy hats hanging side by side. The larger one had a long, pure white feather sticking out from a white, braided-leather hatband. On the floor below the hats were two pairs of brown leather cowboy boots, one large enough for a man, the other pair much smaller. Sheila scowled down at them.

Beyond the pegs, through a wide post-and-beam entrance, she could see most of the living room, with ancient black leather couches and chairs arranged in front of a huge stone fireplace that soared up to a vaulted ceiling.

To the girls' left, a steep staircase of battered wood steps led straight up to the second floor. A wooden handrail, painted white, ran up one side. Sheila gazed up the stairway. Her room was up there at the end of the hall, the room she had slept in almost every night for ten years. She didn't remember it looking so gloomy up there before.

Straight ahead was a bright, wide hallway that led to the kitchen. Neither girl spoke. They stood silent, listening. But they heard nothing. No voices. The only sound was a gentle *tick-tock, tick-tock* of the tall grandfather clock that stood below the stairs.

"Where is everyone?" Katie whispered.

"Who knows? Follow me." Sheila started to walk, one slow step at a time, down the hall, trying not to make a sound. Katie was so quiet Sheila wasn't sure she was still there and glanced over her shoulder. Katie was creeping along, almost stepping on her heels. They tiptoed into the big, old-fashioned kitchen.

Sunlight streamed through wide windows that overlooked the patio and vegetable garden behind the house. White countertops were cluttered with bags of hamburger and hot-dog buns, a package of wieners, jars of relish and mustard, and a couple of paper grocery bags, filled to bursting. A toaster with dry crumbs scattered around it; a coffeemaker containing an inch of coffee, black as grease; a dirty pot on the stove with a wooden spoon sticking out of it; a soggy-looking dishtowel crumpled up near a sink full of dishes. The kitchen smelled like grease, burnt toast and rotten bananas. It never looked, or smelled, like this when Mom was here.

Katie looked at her with a question in her eyes. Sheila shook her head. She had no idea where everyone was. And then she heard the whisper of a sound. Katie heard it too. Sheila nodded in the direction of her father's office, at the end of a short hallway.

Side by side the girls tiptoed toward it.

The two boys stood at the end of the hall, slightly bent at the waist, their ears pressed tight against a closed office door. Sheila and Katie crept toward the boys, who were listening so intently they didn't notice.

Suddenly both boys leapt away from the door and bolted down the hall. Huntley darted between them, but Rusty smashed so hard into Katie she fell over backward, and he crashed to the floor beside her. Her notebook fell open and the two little plastic bags tumbled out just as the office door opened.

5

By the time Sheila's father stepped into the hall, Huntley had reached the kitchen and stood by the counter, calmly removing groceries from a paper bag. Sheila bent over the two cousins, sprawled on the floor at her feet. She scooped up the two little evidence bags and handed them to Katie.

"What's going on here?" her dad demanded. Tall and muscular, he towered over them. He pushed back a tuft of sandy hair that fell across his forehead.

Sheila leaned over Rusty, her arm stretched out in an effort to hide Katie's attempt to stuff the two plastic bags back inside her notebook.

"It's only Rusty." Sheila grabbed Rusty by the wrist and helped him to his feet. "He bumped into Katie and they both fell over. Did I mention he's a bit accident prone?"

For a moment her dad just looked confused. He watched Katie and Rusty walk into the kitchen, Katie shielding her notebook in front of her. Then he scratched his head and turned his attention to Sheila. She was sure he would ask what they were doing outside his office, but all he said was, "Then you'll need to keep him out of trouble. I've got enough to worry about right now without your friends falling off horses or getting run over by cattle."

There were footsteps behind them and two RCMP officers, wearing dark pants with a wide yellow stripe down the sides and beige short-sleeved shirts, emerged from the office. One was as tall as Sheila's dad, over six feet, with huge shoulders and no neck, like a football player. His brown hair was clipped super short, and he had a wide mouth and small, beady eyes. The other man was older, thin and wiry with piercing blue eyes, a long, pointed nose and not much hair on top of his head.

"Shall we go, gentlemen?" Her dad continued down the short hallway with the two Mounties following close behind. Both of them looked glum.

When they heard the front door open, Rusty whispered, "They're going out to search the truck. Your dad said it was okay."

The door shut with a loud clunk and Huntley immediately dropped a pound of butter back into the grocery bag. "Stay here," he told the three of them. "Tell me if they come back in." He charged down the hall.

Katie followed close behind him. Sheila turned to Rusty. "You stay here," she said. "Let us know the second that front door opens."

Rusty nodded and Sheila followed the other two.

The RCMP had left the office door open, and Huntley walked in as if he owned the place. Lagging behind, Sheila glared at the back of his head, but as soon as she stepped into the room, she forgot all about Huntley. Her dad's office hadn't changed a bit. The huge oak desk had once belonged to her great-grandfather, the first Walton born here. As always, the desk was piled high with stacks of papers and unopened envelopes. The brown leather chair behind her dad's desk was as cracked and ugly as she remembered it. Beside the desk, a recycling box overflowed with papers that spilled out onto the floor around it.

Sheila used to be the one who made sure all the recyclables made it to the recycling bins in town at least once a month. She wondered now if some of these papers had been in the box the whole time she was gone.

There, on the computer table behind her dad's desk, was the very same computer she had used to e-mail her friends and research her favorite topic, endangered animals. Especially ones that lived in this area, like grizzly bears.

When the house was built, way back in 1910, this little room off the kitchen had been planned as a spare bedroom for a cook or a maid. Sheila's dad used to tell her about the first Waltons to live here. They arrived from North Dakota to homestead on this quarter of land, and they brought more money with them than most immigrants had in those days. They also brought big plans to be rich landowners, like the "gentleman farmers" they heard about in England. Their dream was to have parties and play tennis and go to picnics and get steadily richer while hired help did all the work for them.

The settlers were in for a shock when it turned out they had to work hard themselves if they were going to make any money at all from a horse and cattle ranch. They may not have hired any cooks or maids, but this room was used by hired ranch hands until the little cottage was built. Since her grandfather's day this room had been an office, but because it started out as a bedroom, it had a closet. And that's where Huntley was right now. Inside the closet.

Katie stood behind him, blocking the doorway. Sheila peered over her shoulder. "He usually locks the door," she said.

But the door to the gun cabinet, inside the closet, was locked as tight as always. It was more like a cage than a cabinet. Thick metal bars, close together, made it impossible to get so much as a hand inside, or to pull a rifle out. Normally there were two rifles in the cabinet, one beside the other. Right now there was only one.

"It's gone all right," Huntley said. "I thought that's what they said, but it was hard to hear through the door. I can't believe it. Chris always keeps the guns locked up in here when he isn't using them."

"I know that," Sheila snapped. Then she said, half to herself, "Maybe he's gone out after wolves or a cougar. Maybe the Mounties came here to help him." Sheila knew as well as anyone that this wasn't true, and she was relieved when neither of them bothered to answer. Her dad had not been carrying a rifle, and the police had definitely not driven all the way out here to help protect the herd. "I wonder if they'll search the rest of the house," she said.

"Nope, he wouldn't let them. I heard him say his daughter just got here after two years away and he was excited to see her. He doesn't want them spoiling her first day home by tearing the place apart. They need a search warrant." As he said this, Huntley walked over to the computer and sat down. He pressed the start-up key.

Sheila smiled to herself. Maybe Dad was happy to see her after all.

Katie crouched in front of the gun cabinet. She opened her notebook and started to write.

"What are you doing?" Sheila asked.

"I examined the lock. There's no evidence of tampering."

"What?"

"It doesn't look like anyone broke in without a key; there are no scratches or anything like that."

"Oh."

Sheila turned her attention to Huntley, now gazing at the computer screen. "What do you think you're doing?"

He didn't answer so she stomped over to him. He placed a blank CD in the holder and slid it shut.

"I asked what you're doing, Huntley."

He glanced up, surprised, as if she had suddenly appeared out of nowhere.

"Thanks for calling me Huntley. I'm making a backup."

"Of what?"

Before he could answer, they heard footsteps running down the hall and Rusty appeared at the doorway. "He's coming back!" he said and disappeared.

Katie shut the closet door. "Let's go!" she started for the hall.

"Shut it down," Sheila told Huntley. "Hurry!"

But it was too late. They heard her father's voice in the kitchen. "Where are the other kids?" he asked Rusty.

Katie hurried to his rescue. "Sheila wanted to show us some game she used to play on your computer."

"Really?" He sounded surprised.

"Yes, something to do with finding habitat for endangered animals. You know, the kind of stuff Sheila likes."

"Oh, okay. Right," he said vaguely. Heavy footsteps crossed the kitchen floor.

Huntley leapt out of the chair and Sheila landed in it. Footsteps clomped down the hall. The computer whirred and clicked, copying e-mail files onto the CD. Suddenly she had a glimmer of an idea of what Huntley was up to. He must figure, like she did, that the Mounties would come back tomorrow with a search warrant. If they did, they might take the computer away. Maybe Huntley knew about some important information stored in the e-mails.

Her dad burst into the room. "Huntley, I asked you to stay out of my office!"

"Uh, I'm sorry, sir, but the door was open and I kind of forgot with all the excitement and all."

"I'm disappointed in you, boy."

Sheila closed the program. She should be pleased that her dad was mad at Huntley, but right now there were more important matters at stake. "It's my fault, Dad," she said, swinging around on the chair. "I remembered a game I used to play, and I wanted to see if it's still here."

"Well?"

"Well what?"

"Is it?"

She swung back to the computer. "I didn't find it," she said honestly. She clicked on "Shut Down" and removed the CD. "And it isn't on this CD either. I guess Huntley thought it might be."

She handed the CD to Huntley. Her dad watched the two of them walk out of his office. He shook his head, mystified.

6

"Why don't you take Katie outside and show her your horse?" her father suggested. "The boys and I will get dinner ready. We can't have you working on your first night at home."

Rusty didn't look completely thrilled about the idea, and Huntley didn't seem exactly ecstatic either. So before either of them could complain out loud, Sheila said, "Thanks, Dad!" and raced for the front door with Katie close behind.

They walked across the farmyard and into the barn. "Ee-ew, it stinks in here!" Katie said, wrinkling her nose.

"I like it," Sheila told her. "It smells like home."

"I'm glad my home doesn't smell like this."

They stopped at Silver's stall. He whinnied softly and put his nose over the gate.

"Isn't he beautiful?" Sheila asked, scratching his muzzle.

"He sure is big!" Katie said.

"What did you expect, a Shetland pony? Haven't you ever seen a horse before?"

"Of course I have!" Katie said, then quietly added, "Just not quite so close up."

"You scared?"

"No! Well, maybe a bit nervous. Sheila, I want to learn how to ride, I just never had a chance before."

"You will tomorrow."

"Good!"

Katie sounded about as enthusiastic as she would if Sheila had invited her to bale hay all day. "Don't worry, we'll find you a good, calm horse."

"Who says I'm worried? But anyway, I checked the gun-cabinet lock and the closet door, and neither of them had been tampered with. What did Huntley find on the computer?"

"I don't know, something to do with e-mails. We'll have to ask him later."

Sheila hadn't finished her last bite of hamburger when her dad leapt up and disappeared toward his office without a backward glance. So that was that. Happy homecoming. Then her ears pricked up. What? She couldn't believe it. Dad's voice, slightly off-key, was singing, "Happy Birthday to you..." The boys and Katie joined in as Dad appeared carrying a big, round chocolate cake with candles flickering.

"I know I'm late," he placed the cake in front of her, "but happy belated birthday, Sheila." He handed her a large plastic bag. "Sorry, I didn't have time to wrap it."

Sheila pulled out a box about fifteen inches long by twelve inches wide. She opened it and there was a brand new Discman, complete with small black earphones and a carrying pouch that had two little round speakers.

"Your mom said you were still using your old Walkman with that huge yellow headset," her dad said. "And look! With this one, if you want to share music with your friends, you can! Just disconnect the earphones and slide it into the pouch."

"Thanks, Dad." Sheila smiled, happy her dad had remembered her birthday. She refused to worry about sharing her music with her friends. That would come later.

"How about you and me go for a ride before it gets dark?" her dad asked after they finished their cake. "I need some quality time with my daughter." He turned to the others. "You three don't mind cleaning up, do you?"

Sheila saw three pairs of eyes take in the mess that engulfed the kitchen. "Of course they don't," she said quickly. "Let's go!"

A little knot of fear lurked in Sheila's belly as she led Silver outside. She hadn't ridden in a long time. What if she couldn't control her horse? Or worse, what if she fell off? Her dad would give her that look he usually reserved for greenhorns. If she couldn't keep up, he would never want to ride with her again. Next time he would take Huntley and leave her at home to wash dishes.

Sheila had learned to ride a small pony when she could barely walk. Then, the spring she turned six, a tiny, long-legged colt was born to her mother's mare, Ingot. He was the color of spun gold, and his little mane and tail shone like silver in the sunshine. Sheila named him Silver and fell in love with him at first sight.

She still remembered that day and how her parents promised he would be her horse. They said her hair was the same color as Silver's mane. She could help raise him, help train him and, when they were both big enough, be the first to ride him. That day came when she was not quite nine years old, and it was the most exciting day of her life.

A year later she had to say good-bye to Silver, her best friend.

Now she ran her fingers through his thick silver mane. Her hair was no longer that color; now it was more like the deep gold of his coat. "Be good for me, okay, Silver?" she whispered.

Once in the saddle, Sheila felt as if she'd never been away. They reached the open range and urged their horses into a gentle canter over rolling, grassy hills. Her dad stayed close beside her on his pale brown gelding, Pita, another name chosen by Sheila.

She glanced sideways at him and was pleased to see that, for the first time since she arrived, her dad was smiling. Then she realized that a huge grin split her own face too. Whatever worries a person might have floated away with the warm breeze in your face and not another human being in sight. "Last one to the stream does all the dishes tomorrow!" she cried and urged Silver to a full gallop.

Her dad raced after her, and the two horses galloped side by side, noses even, until gradually Pita pulled into the lead. But the brown horse stopped suddenly on a low rise. Sheila reined in Silver and followed her father's gaze. Below them, near a copse of lodgepole pine on the far side of a barbed wire fence, were two large portable buildings. A backhoe, bulldozer and SUV were lined up between the portables. Not far away was a huge pile of rocks. Sheila recognized the stream that ran through the compound but could not remember the large, round pond where the stream had been dammed by boulders.

"What's that mess?" she asked in dismay.

Her father was no longer smiling. "The development," he growled.

"But where did it come from? Isn't that the Arnesens' land?"

"It was. They sold ten acres to Glenmar Development a year ago, when Mrs. Arnesen was sick. They needed the money to hire a full-time aide for her."

"But that's not fair!"

"I'm guessing the watchman was shot from somewhere along here." Her dad walked Pita along the low hillside. "Whoever did it would have a perfect view."

"But how would they get here without crossing our land?"

"There's a road from the highway to the development, and a gate down below. But the thing is, anyone who came that way would have to drive right past the night watchman."

"So whoever it was probably came from the other direction, from our place?"

Her dad nodded. "Seems that way."

They rode in silence for a few minutes. It was strange how, as soon as she slowed down, all her worries caught up with her. Her father stopped again. "There's Wendell's place," he said.

Sheila followed her father's gaze to a stand of aspens. On the slope above the stream, on the Walton side of the barbed wire fence, was a brown camper van, almost hidden among the trees.

"Who's Wendell? It looks like he lives there!"

"Wendell Wedman is an old fellow who first showed up about this time last year, down near Swan Pond. Seems he just drove through the gate one day when it was left open and set up camp. He's an interesting old character, and I didn't mind him camping there as long as he didn't cause any trouble. A few days ago I noticed he was back, so I suggested he move to this spot. It's nicer here, especially since our pond dried up. From here he can keep a watch on things for me. Let's go see if he's home."

Sheila followed her dad, wondering about the pond and the pair of trumpeter swans that raised a family there every summer.

Her dad dismounted. "Wendell!" he called. There was no answer. He knocked on the door and waited, but there was no sign of Wendell Wedman.

"I thought the stream was bigger than that," Sheila said, looking down the slope. "What happened?"

"Glenmar Development happened," her dad said bitterly. "They're diverting water for irrigation. They want it for their golf course."

"Golf course? But what about the swans?"

Dad shook his head sadly. "The pond is no more than a bog now."

A big sun glowed orange over the distant mountains as Sheila and her dad rode back into the yard. They were surprised to see Katie and Rusty, each seated on an old brown horse, walking around the corral under Huntley's watchful eye. Katie looked like she was enjoying herself. Rusty clung to the saddle horn as if convinced the horse was about to leap the fence and run through the field with him holding on for dear life.

7

After saying he had tons of paperwork to do, Sheila's dad locked himself in his office. Sheila and the others hurried upstairs to a small bedroom at the front of the house, where Rusty and Huntley would sleep. A dormer window overlooking the yard and barn was only a black square now.

Huntley slid a CD into his laptop computer. "Okay, let's see what we can find out."

"Why did you copy it anyway?" Rusty asked.

"No reason." Huntley clicked on the e-mail icon.

"Aw, c'mon. You don't just sit down and copy e-mails for no reason, especially when you weren't even supposed to be in the office."

"I just thought there might be something from Mom. You know, something important?"

"You mean something to do with the case?" Katie asked.

"What *case*?" Huntley glanced up as if she had lost her mind.

"See, you've gotta understand about Katie," Rusty explained. "Every time something unusual happens, she thinks it's some big *case* for her to solve. She thinks she's the Great Detective."

"Whatever." Huntley stared at the screen. He tapped a few keys. "Here it is!"

From:	Adele James
Date:	July 20, 2005 9:30 PM
To:	Chris Walton
Subject:	Glenmar

Hi Chris:

Well, here I am in the big city again. I'd forgotten how noisy and congested Calgary is! Already the traffic is driving me crazy, and I just got here this afternoon! I can't imagine how I lived in Toronto for so long. But I know for sure I could never move back there after returning to the country. What was I thinking?

I have to admit though, I miss my job as a journalist. No matter. When all of this is settled, I'm going to make more time for my freelance writing.

Thanks again for letting Huntley stay with you. I know he'll be a huge help. I can't believe how well he has adapted to ranch life in just over a year. It must be in his blood, he's a real cowboy now!

I meet with the lawyer tomorrow, wish me luck.

Chris, I'm counting on you to keep an eye on Glenmar Development for me. Last night I dreamt that I came home and they had bulldozed the old homestead to put up a big, ugly clubhouse! Talk about a "While You Were Out!" nightmare!

It's so important to win this battle, I'm really grateful you're here to help. And Mother Nature thanks you too. Think of the grizzlies!

Love,

Adele

For a half second Sheila wondered what grizzly bears had to do with Glenmar Development, but then she focused on those last two words, "Love, Adele," and felt like kicking someone. Huntley for starters.

"There's a reply," Huntley said. He clicked to open another e-mail.

From: Chris Walton

Date: July 20, 2005 10:05 pm

To: Adele James

Subject: RE: Glenmar

Don't worry about anything here at home. I've got everything under control. And, as I mentioned, I've come up with a surefire way of keeping Glenmar off your land, at least for the time being.

We'll talk about it when you get back. Meanwhile, good luck with the lawyer. I'll be thinking of you to-morrow.

I'm off now, onto the range. There are some things I need to take care of. I told Huntley I'd be gone for a few hours. If there's anything he needs, Ben Brown isn't far away. I also told Ben where I'd be, so I expect he'll come up to the house and watch tv. He sure does love my big screen! Anyway, don't worry about Huntley. He's in good hands here and a pleasure to have around.

Must go,

Chris

Sheila glared at the back of Huntley's head. So he was a *pleasure* was he? Isn't that just too precious for words? Obviously *she* wasn't a *pleasure* to have around or her dad might invite her to visit once in a while. "What gives you the right to snoop in other people's e-mails?" she asked crossly.

Huntley looked up in surprise, she sounded so angry. Katie and Rusty both stared at her too.

Her cheeks burned. "I mean, you must have read them earlier or you wouldn't have known they were there. Is that why my dad doesn't want you in his office, because he can't trust you?"

Huntley stared down at his hands. "Kind of," he admitted, "but it's not like you think!"

"You don't know what I think!"

"Okay, then, here's what happened. Before Mom went to Calgary, she and Chris kept talking, you know, about stuff, but they'd stop when I came into the room. I knew something was up, but they wouldn't tell me anything. I don't even know why Mom needs to see a lawyer.

"So, anyway, this morning I got up early and checked my e-mails, but there wasn't one from Mom, even though she promised to send one. Then I came downstairs and Chris wasn't even up yet, which is weird because he's always up way early.

"Anyway, the office door was open so I went in. I guess I sort of clicked on his e-mail and saw there was one from Mom last night. That's when Chris came in, before I even had a chance to read it. He was bursting mad and told me to stay out of his office."

"So why did you copy the e-mails to CD this afternoon?" Katie asked.

"I just...I want to know what's going on. I figured if the police come back and take his computer—like they do on TV—I'd never know what those e-mails said."

"Oh, and I thought you were trying to help!" Sheila said. "But you were just being nosy! Like Katie!"

Sheila felt all jittery inside. She was so angry she couldn't be nice to anyone right now. Huge questions gnawed into her brain. Where did her dad go late last night? And what was his "surefire" way of stopping Glenmar Development? A terrible, sick feeling lurked deep in her stomach, and right now she needed desperately to be alone. She needed time to think. Sheila turned and walked quietly out of the room.

Before she reached her own room, at the back of the house, she heard Katie ask, "I wonder what happened to the rifle."

She closed the door behind her. It felt weird to be in this bedroom again. It hadn't changed much. She and Katie brought some of their stuff in earlier, but this was the first time she had been in here alone. She didn't switch on the light, but stood looking around the room, lit only by soft moonlight that filtered through the window.

Her bed still had the same bedspread, blue with horses galloping all over it. A small bedside table held a lamp and plain white shade, not the frilly one her mother wanted to buy. Her bookcase was strangely empty, except for a couple of cowboy books that belonged to Huntley. She could see them lying there now, and even though she could not see their front covers clearly, she glowered at them. Huntley had been using her room until she arrived. How dare her father give her room to that boy?

She walked over to the tall, rectangular window that looked out toward the foothills. A round moon hung high in the southern sky and lit up a ragged line of snow on the mountain peaks to the west. A shiver ran through her.

Her dad would never hurt anyone, she knew that. But the questions wouldn't leave her alone. *Where was the rifle? What was Dad's surefire plan? Where did he go late last night?*

8

When Sheila opened her eyes the next morning, weak sunlight was just beginning to creep through her window. She hadn't slept much during the night; too many worries made her toss and turn. For hours she lay awake, wishing her room weren't so hot and stuffy, wishing she knew how to help her dad.

Sheila turned her pillow over, squeezed her eyes shut and tried to go back to sleep. She tried to stop thinking, but the worries wouldn't go away, so she tried to form a plan instead. Maybe she should call Mom and ask for help. But Mom would tell her to stay out of it. Or worse. She might insist Sheila come home. No, she wouldn't phone Mom, not yet at least.

Katie would be eager to help, Sheila knew that. And Katie was good at stuff like that, at finding clues and figuring out who the bad guys were. Trouble was,

Katie didn't know when to quit, even if it meant she got herself into a ton of trouble. Now Sheila couldn't decide whether to ask Katie for help or tell her to mind her own business.

Dad couldn't possibly be guilty. Could he? She had not seen much of him in the past two years and, as her mom always said, "People change." Had her dad changed? Was he capable of hurting someone to get what he wanted?

She didn't think so, but how could she be certain? Sheila knew the ranch wasn't doing as well as it used to. Her dad was worried because the price of cattle was way low. Not only that, but the weather seemed to be against ranchers these days. One year it was so hot and dry the grasses on the range and hay in the fields withered and died. The next year it rained so hard everything rotted where it stood. How was he supposed to feed his cattle? How could he keep the horses healthy?

If Dad was afraid of losing the ranch, would that make him do something drastic?

Suddenly Sheila sat up in bed. She could not lie here any longer, worrying until she felt sick to her stomach. Careful not to disturb Katie, she dressed quietly in a purple T-shirt and blue jeans, picked up her shoes and tiptoed from the room.

She padded softly downstairs and left her shoes by the front door. She wanted to go out to the barn and see Silver, maybe even take a ride before anyone else got up, but first she would grab an apple for Silver and one of those fresh, juicy Okanagan peaches for herself.

Her hand was on the fridge door when she heard a noise. She froze, listening. It sounded like a creaky floorboard in the front hall. Good, Dad must be up, maybe they could ride out together. She waited, but no one walked down the hall to the kitchen. Was she imagining things, or did her dad come downstairs and head straight outside?

She grabbed an apple and a peach and closed the fridge door. Retrieving her shoes from the front hall, she pulled the front door open, surprised to see it was not quite latched.

Sheila shivered in the early morning air. The sky shimmered gold over the grasslands to the east, but the sun had not yet risen above the horizon. She shivered again and tried to remember where she left her blue sweatshirt. Was it in the trailer or up in her bedroom?

She hadn't needed it yesterday because the afternoon and evening were so hot. She didn't remember stuffing it into her bag, so it must be in the trailer. Instead of entering the barn, Sheila walked to the trailer and tried the door. It wasn't locked and she stepped inside. At the back were two bunks, one above the other. Sheila's was the top one. She climbed up to look for her sweatshirt.

She found a couple of crumpled T-shirts and a pair of shorts stuffed inside her sleeping bag. Under her pillow was her bathing suit. No sweatshirt. She was about to climb down when she heard a door close. Peeking out through the narrow window beside the bunk, she saw her dad walking down the steps from the house. As she slid from the bunk she noticed Katie's red sweatshirt on the bottom bunk. Something blue stuck out from beneath it. She grabbed her shirt, yanked it over her head and ran outside.

By then Dad was halfway across the yard, heading for the barn. He almost jumped out of his cowboy boots when he saw her. "Sheila! I thought you were asleep upstairs."

"I couldn't sleep. Did you go back inside the house?"

He frowned. "What are you talking about?"

"I heard you go out a few minutes ago. Then I looked out from the trailer and saw you on the steps."

"You're imagining things, girl. A few minutes ago I was in the shower."

His hair was wet and plastered to his head. He smelled lemony, like the shaving cream he always used. Sheila decided the sound she heard must have come from upstairs, not from the front hall as she had thought. "Are you going riding?" she asked.

"Not now. I was coming down to mix up a batch of hotcakes for you kids. But from the bottom step I thought I saw something move out here near the barn, just a glimpse of blue. Anyway, I came out to investigate." He looked at her blue shirt. "Obviously it was you."

"But..."

Her dad slipped an arm around her shoulders. "C'mon, Sheila, let's go make some hotcakes before the hordes descend upon us."

They walked together back toward the house. "Ben and Ryan will be over for breakfast in half an hour. We've got loads of work to do today."

"Ryan's here?"

Dad nodded. "He's in university now, but he's back to help us out for the summer, just like he used to in the old days."

Sheila remembered Ryan well. From the time he was ten, he used to spend his summers on the ranch. He stayed with his father, Ben, in the cottage by a little copse of pines beyond the main house. She never liked the way Ryan teased her, but he often went riding or swimming with her too, kind of like a much older brother.

There was a stack of hotcakes keeping warm in the oven, coffee waiting to be poured and bacon sizzling on the griddle when Ben walked into the kitchen.

"Hey, Sheila!" he greeted her warmly and wrapped her in a big hug. "Sorry I missed you yesterday. I had a load of horseshoeing jobs on some of the ranches down south and didn't get home until late." He stood back. "Let me look at you! You've grown so much, I hardly recognize you, Cowgirl!"

Sheila grinned. For as long as she could remember, Ben had called her Cowgirl and she was glad he hadn't forgotten. Ben had been the Walton's foreman since long before she was born and was almost like an uncle to her. He had a bushy brown-and-gray beard, thin brown hair and, just as she remembered, wore a blue shirt. She wondered if he always wore the very same shirt, or did he have a dozen identical ones?

"You don't look any different," she said.

Then Ryan walked in. "Hi, kiddo!" he winked, grinning. He didn't look like a boy anymore. He was kind of old now, at least twenty, and he was as tall and broad-shouldered as the two older men. Ryan had soft brown hair that lay flat, and his eyes were gray, like his dad's.

"Hi, kiddo, yourself," she said and poured coffee into three mugs.

The men had been gone for hours by the time Katie and the others finally wandered, bleary-eyed, down the stairs. As usual, Katie carried her notebook tucked under her arm, but for once Rusty didn't have his sketchbook.

"It's about time you got up," Sheila said. "I've already had a ride on Silver, and I saddled two quarter horses for you."

"Why?" Rusty's voice held an edge of panic. As if to cover his fear, he babbled on. "What's a quarter horse anyway? If I was going to ride anything—and I'm not saying I will—I'd want the whole horse."

Sheila laughed. So did Huntley, which made her angry, so she stopped abruptly. Katie paid no attention to any of them. She settled at the table, opened her notebook and began to read, one finger following along her lines of notes.

"A quarter horse is a breed of small but really strong and fast horses that know how to outsmart cattle. They're perfect working horses for a ranch."

Rusty looked even more nervous. "They chase your cows?"

"Only when we tell them to," Sheila said. "They're very gentle."

Rusty's eyes appealed to Katie for help, but she was lost in her notes.

"You rode one last night," Huntley said. "You did great."

"I'll take you out on the range today," Sheila suggested. "You'll like it, things haven't changed much in over a hundred years."

A gleam of interest sparked in Rusty's eyes but quickly died. "You mean we'll *walk* out on the range?"

Sheila nodded. "Walk, trot, canter, whatever works."

Rusty turned to his cousin. "Katie? Are you listening to this? They're trying to get us killed! They're putting us on fast, cow-chasing horses and riding out to the range where there's—surprise—cows!"

Sheila noticed that Rusty said *they* instead of *she,* as if he automatically assumed Huntley would come too. She glared at Huntley.

Katie placed her finger under a line in her notebook and looked up slowly. "We need to visit the scene of the crime," she said.

Rusty groaned.

9

As much as she longed to tap Silver with her heels and take off at a gallop across the rolling, grass-covered hills, Sheila knew she couldn't. Silver tossed his head and snorted impatiently, so bursting with energy Sheila could scarcely hold him back. But she remembered what her father said about her friends getting hurt and reminded herself how accident-prone Rusty really was, and she tightened the reins.

Sheila had not spoken one word to Huntley to-day, but he didn't appear to mind, or even notice for that matter, which was a bit depressing. However, he did seem to understand the need to hold the horses back—maybe he had seen Rusty in action already.

She studied Huntley. He seemed comfortable in the saddle, riding his black-as-midnight horse, but she didn't know why he had to wear a black cowboy hat, same as her dad's. At least it didn't have a white, braided-leather band and white feather. Sheila remembered braiding those three long leather strips and placing the band on Dad's black hat for a Father's Day surprise.

She had found the white wing feather later that summer, during the molting season of the trumpeter swans. Sheila used to sit by Swan Pond and watch them for hours, a beautiful pair that raised their little brood here on the ranch every year. Again she wondered if they had returned this spring. Without Swan Pond, where would they go? Maybe Huntley knew. Too bad she wasn't speaking to him.

It took forever to reach the hill above the development, but at last they reined in the horses. "This is where my dad figures a sniper would have stood," Sheila said.

"How do I get down?" Katie asked. She stared at the ground near her horse's feet as if she were perched high on a rooftop.

Sheila made an effort not to roll her eyes. She glanced at Huntley; he better not be smirking!

He wasn't. "Wait there, I'll help you," he said and slid down from his horse before Sheila could say a word. That boy was so pushy she felt like screaming. Katie was *her* friend, not his. Wasn't he content to take her dad away? Did he want her friends too? She swung down from Silver and marched over to help Rusty before he fell. Or before Huntley got there to help him first.

She held Rusty's horse. "Keep your left leg in the stirrup," she told him. "Hang onto the saddle horn and swing your right leg over the horse. Good, now slip your left foot out of the stirrup before you..."

Rusty crashed to the ground and the horse twitched uneasily, but Sheila held on fast. Rusty gazed up at her, his head and shoulders lying in the long grass, his left leg in the air, foot stuck in the stirrup. Sheila was about to ask if he was hurt when he grinned.

"That's why you take your foot out first," she said, "before you slide to the ground."

"Now you tell me!" Rusty said.

To Sheila's annoyance, Huntley rushed over and freed Rusty's foot. "Thanks," Rusty said. He picked up his baseball cap and scrambled to his feet, brushing dry dirt and bits of brown grass from his shirt.

Sheila grinned to herself, watching Rusty and Huntley walk to the edge of the rise. Rusty walked weird, his legs stiff and his knees stuck out sideways as if he still sat astride his horse. Horseback riding used muscles Rusty probably didn't even know that he had.

Already Katie was busy scouting around. Nose hovering close over the ground, she searched the grass for clues. For once she had left her notebook behind, along with her backpack. Sheila had told her she would have enough to worry about on this first ride without any extra weight or straps on her back. Katie stopped, studied something that lay in the brown grass, then straightened up and reached into the back pocket of her jeans. She pulled out a tiny notepad with a small pencil stuck through its coil binding. Flipping it open, she started to write.

Sheila marched over to Katie. "What are you writing?"

"I found a cigarette butt." She whipped a small plastic bag from her other back pocket and scooped up the butt. "C'mon, let's see what else we can find."

Sheila felt a sudden surge of interest. Maybe Katie was onto something. Her dad didn't smoke anymore. He used to when she was little, but he quit because Mom told him cigarette smoke was bad for children's lungs.

Working together, the girls searched the full length of the ridge. In one spot the grass was trampled down as if someone had sat there. On the flattened grass they found several more cigarette butts and a matchbook with the name of a Calgary restaurant printed on it. They picked each item up with a plastic bag, careful not to touch it. Sheila felt like a crime-scene investigator, like the ones she sometimes saw on TV.

They walked down a gentle slope toward the stream and across the muddy ground near the water's edge. A row of aspen trees, their wafer-thin green leaves trembling in a slight breeze, lined the bank. "Look!" Katie said.

A set of wide tire tracks led up to the aspens and sank deeper into the soft mud to form a V shape. The tracks swung in a semicircle to the right, formed a second V, then headed straight for the grassy slope. Two swaths of flattened grass led up and over the low ridge.

Sheila watched in dismay as Katie collected a sample of the mud and a twig from an aspen tree.

"What're you kids doin' here?" a gruff voice yelled.

Sheila jumped. Several feet behind them stood a rail-thin old man. Narrow slits of blue eyes stared intensely out beneath bushy white eyebrows. His pure white hair stood up straight on top of his head as if he never bothered to comb it. Spiky gray whiskers protruded from his jutting chin.

"Well?" he demanded. "Who are you?"

"Who are you?" Katie demanded right back. "And what are you doing here? This is Sheila's dad's land, not yours."

The man's eyebrows shot up, and he narrowed his blue eyes to study Sheila more closely. "You Sheila?"

She nodded.

"How come you don't look like your pop?" he snapped.

Sheila tried to think of an answer that made sense, but was saved when the boys ran up.

"Hey, Wendell!" Huntley said. "What happened? Looks like there's nobody down at the development."

Wendell Wedman turned to Huntley. "How should I know? Guess they got scared off after the shootin' an' all. Can't say as I blame 'em, and good riddance if you ask me."

"Do you live here?" Katie asked, looking at a brown van halfway up the slope behind them and partially hidden by aspen trees.

"As a matter of fact, I'm stayin' here for the summer. Chris asked me to keep an eye on them guys and call him if they stray off their own land. So you might call me the night watchman for the Triple W." He chuckled. "And you could say two of those Ws belong to me. Time was, I used to call myself Double W."

"Or Dub-Dub for short," Rusty grinned.

Wendell gave him an odd look.

"So, then, what did you see on the night of the shooting?" Katie asked, her pencil poised above the little notebook.

Wedman's face seemed to close up. He looked away. "Nothin' much."

"Did you see a truck?"

"Could be."

"Was it an old, blue pickup?"

"Couldn't say for sure."

"Did you see anyone up on the ridge?"

"Could be."

"Wendell, you told me you saw a truck," Huntley said. "Did you see anything else?"

Wendell rubbed his fingers through his white hair until it stood up even higher than before. He shifted from one foot to the other. "Saw your pop," he said to Sheila.

"You saw him before the shooting?" Katie asked.

"Naw. The shooting woke me up from a sound sleep, darn near gave me a heart attack. Dog started barkin' like he'd gone mad. When I looked out he was runnin' for his truck."

"Your dog has a truck?" Rusty asked.

Wendell frowned. "Chris was running, the dog

was barking," he said slowly and clearly for Rusty's benefit. As if to demonstrate, a big, shaggy, black dog came bursting out of the trees, barking loudly. "Hush now, Rebel," Wendell ordered and the dog sat down obediently.

"Wasn't it dark out?" Katie asked.

"Sure was, it was the middle of the night!"

"Then how could you tell it was Sheila's dad?"

"Simple. The moon was hangin' above them mountains. I recognized his hat. That white feather of his showed up clear as day."

"Why didn't you tell me this before?" Huntley asked.

Wendell shrugged. "Don't want to cause trouble. Happens I like Chris Walton. Can't say the same for the Coutts."

"What coots?" Sheila asked.

"The ones set on wreckin' this place, Glen and Marla Coutts. They're a husband-and-wife team who won't be happy until this entire province is plastered in golf courses, houses and shoppin' malls."

"Glenmar Development," Huntley said. "Get it? 'Glen-Mar.'"

Sheila's stomach twisted. This man, Wendell, liked her dad and didn't like Glenmar Development. So, if he said he saw Dad up here the night before last, then it must be true. "Let's go riding," she said and walked away.

10

That evening they sat around the picnic table on the patio outside the kitchen, eating barbecued ribs and corn on the cob. There were a lot of chewing and swallowing noises, but no one spoke. It seemed to Sheila that they were each mulling over worries of their own. For sure she was.

When they returned from their ride that afternoon, she had made Katie promise not to ask Dad any questions, not so much as one. Katie had nodded tersely and hobbled off to soak in a hot bath. It seemed like Katie still wasn't speaking to her, but Sheila didn't care. As long as Katie kept her mouth shut, she couldn't pester Dad with questions.

Rusty was having trouble staying awake. He sat very still on a big soft pillow and leaned his elbows on the table. His eyes kept drooping shut, but he still managed to eat his share of the food.

Huntley simply stared at his plate and ate slowly, as if he felt sick or sad or something. He had been quiet for hours. Maybe he finally figured out that Sheila wasn't talking to him. All good.

For her part, Sheila tried to avoid looking at her dad. In spite of making Katie promise to be quiet, she could barely keep her own mouth shut. In her mind she kept hearing Wendell's words. *I recognized his hat. That white feather of his showed up clear as day.*

At the same time she couldn't forget what her dad said in his e-mail to Adele. *I'm off now, onto the range. There are some things I need to take care of.* And that was right after he told Adele he had figured out a "surefire" way of keeping Glenmar Development off her land.

Sheila wanted to ask where he went and what this surefire method was, but how could she? He would know right away they had been snooping in his e-mail. "We met Wendell Wedman today," she said.

Chewing and swallowing ceased. Everyone stared at her, mouths gaping, mouths shut tight, butter dripping from chins. Eyes shifted to her dad. He had been gazing toward the mountains, but now he turned slowly to face Sheila. His eyes looked cloudy. "What?"

She had gone that far, now she had no choice but to go on. "We rode out to see the development and we met Wendell Wedman."

"Oh. Good. I was a bit worried when he wasn't there last night. I'm beginning to think it was a mistake to let him stay in that spot. And he never checks his cell-phone messages, so I was going to ride out and check on him later. How is the old fella?"

"Fine." Sheila tried to leave it at that but somehow the words in her mind slipped out of her mouth on their own. "He says he saw you up there the night before last."

"What?" Dad looked surprised. "He's crazy! I was nowhere near the south fence. I took Pita and rode in the opposite direction, up to the open range. Some of the ranchers have been losing cattle to a wolf pack up that way, so I thought I'd take advantage of an almost full moon to ride up and check on our herd."

That made perfect sense. Sheila started to feel better.

"Did you take a rifle with you?" Katie asked.

Sheila glared at her, but Katie didn't notice, or pretended not to notice, and added, "I mean, if you thought there were wolves, you would take a rifle, wouldn't you?"

"As a matter of fact I did."

"Did you shoot anything?"

He shook his head. "No."

"Then what?"

Dad frowned. Sheila could see he was getting annoyed, and she glared at Katie more fiercely. When that didn't work she tried to find Katie's shin with the toe of her running shoe, to give her a warning kick. But Katie must have tucked her feet under the bench in anticipation.

"What do you mean?" Dad asked.

"Did you put the rifle back when you were done?"

"Of course! It would be irresponsible to leave a rifle where someone else could come across it."

Tension around the table rose. Sheila hoped Katie would have enough sense to keep quiet now.

Amazingly, she did. But Sheila's dad continued anyway. "The thing that really worries me, though, is that my other rifle is missing, and Ben insists he hasn't used it. It's not like either of us to leave a gun unaccounted for." He looked sternly at each of them in turn. "If any of you kids see that rifle, I want you to promise not to touch it. Just come and find me or Ben."

"Or Ryan?" Sheila asked.

Her dad nodded. "Yes. Ryan is very responsible around guns."

After dinner Sheila hoped her dad would ask her to go riding again, so she was disappointed when he stood up and carried his dishes to the kitchen. Her spirits lifted when he returned and stuck his head out the door. "Will you kids please clean up the kitchen? I've got work to do."

He closed the door again and disappeared in the direction of his office.

As soon as he was gone, Katie whipped out her notebook and started to write. Sheila leaned across the table, trying to read upside down. Katie looked up, gave her a withering look and placed her left arm in front of her book.

"Remind me never to ride a horse again as long as I live," Rusty moaned. "Every muscle in my body aches!" He rested his head on his folded arms and closed his eyes.

Huntley stood and picked up the dirty plates. Sheila felt like tripping him. Why did he always have to be the perfect kid?

Sheila fell asleep exhausted that night. When she jerked suddenly awake, her room was dark, not a glimmer of moonlight at her window. She stared into the blackness, her heart beating too fast. Had she heard something? Or was she dreaming?

The noisy clatter of a truck starting up lingered in her mind, but was it real or unreal? The sound was mixed with her dream. She was out near the development, looking at those tire tracks, when Wendell Wedman came swooping down the hill in his van, headed straight for her. That's what made her wake so suddenly. Or was it? Her thoughts were clouded, her eyes were heavy, she couldn't stay awake.

Next time Sheila heard an engine, she opened her eyes to a room filled with early-morning sunlight. There was a crunch of tires on gravel at the front of the house. The engine shut off, a door slammed, then another. She glanced at Katie, but all that showed of her was a lumpy sheet. Sheila slipped out of bed and scrambled to get dressed.

11

Sheila started down the stairs barefoot. She stopped at the sound of a voice. More than one, hushed, as if the speakers did not wish to be overheard. The front door closed with a quiet click.

"This way, gentlemen," her dad said.

Footsteps moved along the hall toward the kitchen.

Sheila crept down the remaining steps. Clutching the bottom post with one hand, she leaned out to see around the grandfather clock. The back of her dad's head was almost hidden by two men who followed close at his heels. They both wore RCMP uniforms.

Sheila's heart leapt. Her breath caught in her throat. How did Dad get downstairs so fast? How did he know the police were here? They never did knock on the door.

"I just made some coffee. Would you like some?" Dad's voice drifted down the hall, barely audible.

The two men mumbled something that might have been yes. Mugs clinked, the carafe clunked on the counter, the fridge door opened and shut. Then all three men shuffled down the short hall to her dad's office. The door closed.

Sheila swallowed. She wished Katie were awake. Katie would tiptoe right down that hall, put her ear to the office door and listen to every word.

Okay, but Sheila could do the same thing by herself, couldn't she?

Just then a hand touched hers on the post. A quick, light touch and then it was gone. Sheila stifled a scream. She looked up, expecting to see Katie, but it wasn't her friend's face that gazed down at her, it was Huntley's.

"What are you doing here?" she snapped.

"Same as you," Huntley whispered. "I couldn't sleep, I was worried about Chris, then I heard a car outside so I got up and looked out. It's the police."

"I know, they're in Dad's office."

"Want to go listen at the door?"

Sheila almost said no, she did not need Huntley's help. But just moments ago she was wishing Katie were here so she wouldn't feel so horribly alone.

Huntley simply stood there, waiting for her answer and looking as miserable as she felt. If she told him to mind his own business, would he?

Maybe. But, then again, maybe this was his business too. If her dad was involved in something bad, then his mom was probably part of it too. "Okay," she whispered and they tiptoed down the hall together.

They pressed their ears to the office door.

"Where were you last night?" asked a police officer.

"Right here."

"You mean right here in this house?"

"No, I mean right here in this office. I slept in here because I'm worried about that missing rifle. I figure if someone got in once, they might come back."

"And just who might that be?"

"I lay awake half the night thinking about that. No one around here would be careless enough to not lock up a rifle after use."

"Are you sure you didn't use it yourself?"

"Of course I'm sure. When I take a gun out, I always return it as soon as I get home. I lock it up before doing anything else."

"I see." The officer sounded like he didn't believe a word. "So you haven't seen the missing rifle?"

"No. I had this one out the same night as the shooting. As I told you before, I took it with me out to the range where wolves have been reported."

"I see," the same cynical voice said. "And exactly where did you say these wolves are?"

"North of here, on the open range. They've been killing our cattle."

"Who, besides you, has access to the gun cabinet?" a deeper voice asked.

"Only Ben, my foreman. He sometimes needs a rifle for the same reason I do, to scare predators away from the herd."

"And Ben wasn't using this other rifle on the night in question?"

"No, he was here. I asked him to stay in the house with Huntley."

"Huntley?"

"Huntley James. The boy who's staying with me while his mother is in Calgary."

"I see," the first voice said. "And Huntley's mother would be Adele James, the owner of the land in question?"

"She is."

"Well, Mr. Walton, this time we brought a search warrant. We got it early this morning, after the fire. I'm afraid we'll need to search your house and property. We'll be taking the rifles in question at this time. You might want to get those kids out of bed upstairs before we search their rooms."

Chairs creaked as the men got to their feet. Huntley pulled at Sheila's sleeve.

But Sheila didn't move. She wanted to hear the answer to the question she hoped her dad would ask. He did.

"What fire?"

"Haven't you heard? There was a fire over at the development last night. One of the buildings was destroyed and the fire chief believes it was arson. I don't suppose you were up that way around three o'clock this morning?"

"I told you, I was right here."

"Alone?"

"If you're asking whether I have an alibi, no, I don't."

"Mr. Walton, if you don't mind waking those kids up, we'd like to begin our search now."

Sheila and Huntley fled to the kitchen.

A moment later the office door opened and closed. Her dad walked into the kitchen, rubbing one hand over his stubbly chin and studying the floor at his feet.

"Hi, Dad!"

His head jerked up. "Sheila! Huntley! I didn't know you were awake!"

Sheila had pulled the fridge door open and stuck her head inside. She reached for the orange juice. Huntley opened a drawer, looked inside and closed it again. "Yep," he said, "yep, we're up all right."

Sheila shut the fridge door. "Were you working in your office all night?"

"I...Listen, kids, there's something I need to tell you. Come sit at the table."

Sheila's heart pounded so hard it hurt as she crossed to the table and sat down. She clutched the jug of orange juice in both hands. Was her dad about to confess?

But he only told them the police were in his office with a search warrant and explained why. Sheila and Huntley listened politely and nodded occasionally, as if they knew nothing about it. When he was done, Dad said, "You'd better go upstairs and wake your friends."

Sheila and the others sat at the kitchen table, eating cereal and watching the two police officers walk past carrying stacks of papers. They even took the recycling bin. Just as Huntley had predicted, they took the computer and then returned for the rifles.

While the police searched upstairs, the kids went outside. They stopped near the police vehicle. "We need to watch them," Katie whispered, "and see what they take."

"Sure, but we can't just stand here and stare," Rusty said.

"No," Sheila agreed. "But we could watch from the corral. How about Huntley and I give you guys a riding lesson?"

Rusty turned pale. "I don't think so," he said. "Besides, we already know how to ride. We spent all day in the saddle yesterday, remember?"

"Well, yeah," Sheila nodded. "But the police don't know that. Besides, you could use some practice trotting."

"Oh man!" Rusty groaned.

"How about you two give us a demonstration?" Katie suggested. She seemed as hesitant as Rusty.

Sheila and Huntley looked at one another. They both grinned. "Okay," Sheila said, "but only if you admit you're a little bit sore from yesterday."

"A little?" Rusty asked. "I may never again sit down without pain!"

They all turned to Katie. "Okay, I admit it, I have a sore butt! If it means I don't have to ride today, I'll admit to just about anything. Besides, I need to take notes."

While Sheila and Huntley put their horses through their paces, Katie and Rusty took up positions on the fence where they could watch the riders, the front door and the police vehicle. But the results were disappointing. The men came outside carrying large bags that they placed in the back of their SUV. It was impossible to tell what was inside the bags.

Sheila was trotting Silver around the corral when the Mounties walked over to her dad's truck. The thinner man leaned inside and lifted something from the floor. He passed it to his partner, then leaned inside again. Sheila pulled her horse up short. The Mountie returned to his vehicle carrying a red plastic gasoline container.

Sheila's stomach turned over when the second Mountie followed, carrying a rifle at his side. Sheila tapped Silver's sides until he broke into a canter.

12

Sheila slowed Silver to a walk and tried not to watch the white SUV drive slowly down the long driveway, but she couldn't pull her eyes away. She was afraid it would stop, reverse and come roaring back to the house, lights flashing and siren wailing.

She held her breath when it stopped at the road. Her hands fidgeted with the reins. Then the police vehicle made a right turn. Flashes of white appeared and disappeared along the row of pines that lined the fence until finally it was out of sight.

Sheila's stomach fluttered as she walked Silver to the barn door and dismounted. She led him through the wide doorway, knowing Huntley had stopped near the fence where Katie and Rusty stood. She refused to look at them. They would be all sorry and sympathetic, they would smile and try to cheer her up. If only they would simply go away, she could handle that much better.

Sheila knew exactly what they were thinking, and she couldn't blame them. They thought her dad was guilty. Maybe she should climb back up on Silver and ride away. Take off across the grasslands where she wouldn't need to talk to anyone. She patted Silver's neck, but she didn't feel like riding, not anymore.

Sheila removed Silver's saddle and bridle and put them in the tack room. The horse didn't need grooming, but she stood beside him anyway and brushed his thick silver mane.

"At least *you* don't think he's guilty, do you, Silver?"

"Who's guilty?"

Katie's voice, so close behind, made Sheila jump. "I wish you wouldn't sneak up on me like that!" Sheila snapped.

"I didn't mean to sneak. I just walked across the barn like a normal person. I thought you knew I was here. I thought you were ignoring me again."

"What do you want?"

"Nothing, Sheila—I just want to talk to you." Katie hesitated. "You okay?"

"What do you think?" Sheila growled. She ran the brush through Silver's mane.

"I think it's time we got busy," Katie said.

Outside, Huntley was trying to convince Rusty to go for a short horseback ride down to the swimming hole.

"I'm not riding anywhere," Rusty insisted. "How about I walk and meet you there?"

At the fence, Sheila listened and thought how good a swim would feel. The sun already beat down hard, and a hot, dry wind stirred dust into the air. She turned to ask Katie what she wanted to do, but Katie wasn't there.

A flash of white caught her eye, and she spotted Katie's T-shirt and red shorts just disappearing behind the cottonwoods. Sheila ran and caught up to her on the lane that led around the grove of tall trees.

"Where are you going?"

"To question the foreman."

"What? Ben? You can't question him!"

"Why not?" Katie didn't stop, didn't even slow down.

"Because it's not like he's just a ranch hand; he's more like a friend or...something." Sheila struggled to find words that would convince Katie to give up this stupid idea. She didn't want Katie to go stomping into Ben's house and accuse him of something he didn't do. Ben might not mind shooting animals, but he was no more likely to shoot at a person than her dad was. For as long as Sheila could remember, Ben had lived here. He helped her learn to ride and train Silver.

"I'm not going to question him, exactly," Katie said. "I just want to find out if he knows anything."

"Don't you think he would have told us by now?"

"Maybe, maybe not. Sometimes witnesses don't realize they saw something important until you question them."

"So Ben's a witness now?"

"Could be."

The cottage looked a lot like the main house, but on a smaller scale. It was painted white, with a covered porch across the front. Its steep roof had two dormer windows that made it look as if there were bedrooms upstairs, but Sheila knew there was only a loft up there, where Ben had his office.

They reached the front door—still green, Sheila was pleased to see. She lifted the door knocker, shaped like a horse's head, and tapped four times.

A minute later the door swung open and Ben stood on the threshold, grinning down at them. "So this is your friend Katie?"

Sheila nodded.

"Pleased to meet you, Katie." He shook her hand. "Any friend of Sheila is a friend of mine. Come on in, girls. I was just finishing my coffee in the kitchen. Ryan's gone to the city for a couple of days, left last night."

Just as in the main house, to the right of the front door was a row of pegs for jackets, a top shelf for hats and a low shelf for boots. Ben's old, brown winter jacket hung on one peg, a brown leather vest on another. There was one cowboy hat, light brown, on the top shelf. Sheila smiled to see that it still had the leather band she braided for Ben the same year she made the white one for her dad. Ben's was brown of course. It seemed everything Ben owned, other than his work shirt, was brown. Even his last name was Brown.

She wondered if Ryan liked brown as much as his father did. Ryan used to wear a cowboy hat the same as his dad's, but it was probably too small for him now. Come to think of it, she hadn't noticed him wearing a hat.

The living room and dining area to the right were flooded with light from one of the dormers above. The door on their left was closed, but Sheila knew it was Ben's bedroom. Behind his room, along a short hall that ran behind a steep ladder-like stairway to the loft, was the bathroom, and beyond that was Ryan's room at the back of the house. They followed Ben through the wide-open living room and dining area to a small kitchen.

Ben's kitchen might be tiny, but it was as neat as a kitchen can be. Unlike Sheila's dad, Ben always insisted that everything be in its place. His coffee mug sat on the counter in front of a high stool with a newspaper neatly folded by it. The coffeepot was already washed and sat gleaming on the coffee machine.

"Have a seat, girls." Ben waved at the two high stools in front of the counter.

"Uh...if you don't mind, I'd rather stand," Katie said, eyeing the hard wooden stool.

"Suit yourself." Ben smiled knowingly, winked at Sheila and then said, "I've got some chocolate milk. Do you still like it as much as you used to, Cowgirl?"

"Sounds good," Sheila said, although she didn't feel like drinking anything right now, with the way her stomach was leaping around. She worried Katie would embarrass her or hurt Ben's feelings, or both.

Katie stood at the end of the counter and flipped open her notebook. She thanked Ben for the chocolate milk and ate one of the graham wafers spread with peanut butter Ben put on a plate.

Ben perched on the stool next to Sheila, sipped his coffee, put the mug down and asked, "Why do I get the feeling you two aren't simply here for the pleasure of my company?"

Sheila almost choked on her chocolate milk. How

did he know? What should she say? "Katie thinks you might know something you don't know you know," she told him.

"How can I know it if I don't know I know it?" Crinkles fanned out from Ben's eyes.

Sheila tried to laugh, but she suddenly felt like crying. She stared at her chocolate milk, wrapped her fingers around the cold, frosty glass and waited for someone else to speak because there was a lump in her throat that made talking impossible.

"The thing is, Mr. Brown..."

"Please, call me Ben! Nobody calls me Mr. Brown, makes me sound like a politician—or a criminal," he chuckled.

Katie smiled politely. "The thing is, Ben, that you were there on the night in question..."

"What question...sorry, bad habit. I promise not to interrupt again."

"The night the night watchman was shot," Katie explained, "you were up at the house, right?"

Ben nodded.

"So you might have seen something important to the case. Can you please tell me what happened, in your own words?"

"Well, I generally tend to use my own words on account of whose would I use if I didn't use mine?"

Ben slapped his hand to his forehead. "Oops! Sorry again." He took a deep breath, sipped his coffee and stared out the window. A moment later he said, "Okay, here's how it went. Chris called me about ten thirty on the *night in question*. Said he was worried about the calves up on the range to the north. Apparently our neighbor up that way called about some problem with wolves."

He spoke slowly, a half smile on his face, while Katie scribbled in her notebook.

"I asked if he wanted me to ride along, and he said he'd be fine, but he was concerned about leaving young Huntley on his own. I was about ready to turn in, but said I'd come on up to the house, there's a movie I've been wanting to watch on his big-screen TV. And that's what I did."

"Was Chris there when you arrived?" Katie asked.

Ben shook his head. "Nope, didn't see him, must have just left."

"What about the truck?"

Ben frowned. "The truck? Can't recall. I assumed he'd taken Pita though. That's rough terrain for his old beater."

"Then what?"

"Well, let's see." He rubbed a hand over his chin. "I zipped upstairs to see if Huntley wanted to watch the movie, but he was already sawing logs, he'd put in a full day's work—he's a good worker, that boy."

Sheila scowled and sipped her chocolate milk.

"Then I made myself some coffee so I could stay awake. I went to the living room, slipped my video in the machine and settled on the couch."

"Did you watch the whole movie?"

"You kidding? Have you tried that couch? It's so soft you feel like you're floating in the clouds. And I'd been working hard since six o'clock that morning. Don't think I got through ten minutes before I nodded off. Never touched my coffee. Next thing I knew, the back door creaked open and I leapt off the couch. Couldn't believe it was after two already!"

"Was it Chris?"

"Chris? At the door?" He shook his head. "That's what I figured at first."

"So who was it?"

"Turned out to be Ryan, my son. He came looking for me, said he got worried when I was so late."

"Does he have keys for the house?"

"I generally leave all the keys right there," he nodded at a row of key hooks beside the door, "but I took them with me that night. Ryan found a key for the back door he used as a kid. That's why he came in that way, he took the shortcut to the back of the house."

"Then what?"

"Uh...let me think. I went into the hall to meet Ryan, we talked for a minute and then I went back to shut off the TV. Ryan offered to stay at the house until Chris came home."

"And? Did he?"

"No need. That's when Chris arrived at the front door. We said goodnight and wandered on home."

"So you both went out the front door?"

"Yep."

"Did you notice the truck then?"

"As a matter of fact, yes. It was there all right. I remember because it was pinging away like it does when it cools. Sounded way louder in the quiet night."

"Which means the truck had been running," Katie said, making a careful note.

"Well, yeah, I guess you're right. I was too sleepy to think about it at the time, but now you mention it, I guess I did know something I didn't know I knew!"

13

Worse and worse. Everything they learned made her dad look guiltier. If he went out in the truck that night, then...she couldn't think about it right now. With her thumb, Sheila traced a big "x" in the condensation on her chocolate milk glass and vaguely heard Katie ask to use the bathroom.

"Sure thing, just down the hall next to Ryan's room." Ben nodded in that direction.

Katie closed her notebook, placed her pen and empty glass on top, gave Sheila a warning glance and left the room.

Sheila wondered what that was about.

"Your friend fancies herself a detective, does she?" Ben asked after they heard the bathroom door close.

Sheila nodded. "Katie manages to stumble across a mystery everywhere she goes, like she's some kind of bad-luck charm." She stared at her hands, fingers locked together on the countertop. "I should never have brought her here."

"What? Sheila, whatever happens has been in the works for a long time and would have happened no matter who came visiting. But if you ask me, you've got to keep that girl in check before someone gets hurt!"

"Ben, you don't think my dad did it?"

"Chris? Shoot at someone? Are you kidding? That man doesn't even like to shoot a wolf. He'll only kill one as a last resort."

"You and I know that, but the police think he's guilty. A truck just like his was spotted near the development on the *night in question*. Then, today, his missing rifle showed up in the truck."

"What?" Ben plunked his mug down so hard, drops of coffee bounced over the top. "Are you sure?"

Sheila nodded. "The police found it. And a gas can too! Now you say Dad's truck was out that night." As soon as she said this, Sheila gasped. She had suddenly remembered half waking the night before and thinking she heard a truck start up.

Ben placed his rough, callused hand over Sheila's and gave it a comforting pat. "Now, don't you worry. Everything will work out for the best, you'll see."

He glanced at his watch. "Do you think Katie has set up camp in the bathroom?"

As he said this, Sheila thought she heard a soft footstep in the hall. Then the bathroom door opened and Katie strolled back toward the kitchen.

"Show me this shortcut," Katie said when they were outside.

Sheila led the way to a narrow path that cut straight through the cottonwoods.

Once on the path, Katie stopped and bent over her notebook.

"What are you writing?" Sheila asked.

"Just a note about what I saw."

"In Ben's cottage?"

Katie nodded. "In Ryan's room."

"You went into Ryan's room? You're not supposed to do that. How nosy can you get? How would you like someone snooping around in your room? You don't even like it if anyone reads your notebook!"

Katie shrugged. "That's personal. This is an investigation."

"So? What did you see?"

"Only a black cowboy hat. It's on the shelf in his closet."

Sheila felt a burst of hope. "And? Did it have a white band? Was there a feather?"

"No," Katie admitted. "Not that I could find."

Her hopes sank. "Do you know how many black cowboy hats are in Alberta?"

The path ended at the back patio, but neither of them felt like going inside just yet, so they continued to the front of the house. Both girls stopped abruptly. At first glance Sheila thought the RCMP had returned, and her heart crashed into her stomach with a sickening thud. Then she realized the white SUV parked beside her dad's old blue truck was tiny compared to the RCMP vehicle. On the door was a blue decal in the shape of a horseshoe with bright red lettering around its inside edge. The girls moved closer to read the words "Cottonwood Creek Ranch."

"That's the Arnesens' ranch," Sheila said, "where Huntley lives now."

"The car must belong to his mom," Katie said. "She must be back from Calgary."

They both turned to the house, its red door thrown wide open. They glanced at one another, then hurried across the yard, up the steps and through the door. The house stood cool and silent as they paused in the front hall. They walked quietly toward the kitchen.

A woman wearing a bright red T-shirt and dark blue shorts sat at the table with her back to the girls.

Her shining, soft brown hair was pulled back in a ponytail that brushed the back of her neck. Her legs were crossed at the knee, a flat-soled red sandal dangled from the toes of her right foot and her toenails were painted red. The woman was eating a sandwich and concentrating on a sheet of paper covered in small print. A short stack of similar papers lay on the table in front of her.

"Where's my dad?" Sheila demanded.

The woman's arms jerked, her foot hit the floor and she swung around. "I was wondering the same thing!" she said. She stood up then and smiled. Her teeth were very straight and very white. Sheila thought they gleamed like a toothpaste commercial. She had a round face and round blue eyes. In fact, she was round all over, no taller than Sheila and way shorter than Sheila's mom. "You must be Sheila," the woman said, still showing her teeth. "I recognize you from your pictures. Your dad sure misses you."

"Oh," Sheila said. Nothing else came to mind so she simply stood there studying this woman and wondering why she kept smiling as if her face was permanently stuck that way. Probably to show off her dimples. Sheila detested dimples.

"I'm Adele James. Have you met my son, Huntley?"

Sheila shrugged. Seemed fairly obvious.

"Hi," Katie said, "I'm Katie, Sheila's best friend."

"Yes, Chris told me you were here. You and your brother, Russell?"

"Rusty. He's my cousin."

"So do you girls know where Huntley is? I just got here a half hour ago and haven't seen a soul."

"I think Huntley and Rusty went swimming," Katie said. "He didn't know you were coming back today."

Adele looked confused. "Now that's odd. I asked Chris to tell him. When I phoned yesterday, Huntley was out riding with you kids."

She turned to Sheila. "Your dad said he'd be here when I got back. Any idea where he is?"

Sheila shook her head. "He was here when we left. He's probably out riding." She didn't mention her dad liked to take off on long rides when he had something on his mind, and she was pretty sure he had tons on his mind right now.

"I checked. Pita is in the barn."

Sheila glanced out the window. Wherever Dad went, it was his own business and not this Adele person's.

"I'm sure he'll be back soon." Adele smiled again. "Would you girls like toasted cheese sandwiches?"

Sheila glanced toward the stove. A greasy frying pan with a pancake flipper sticking from it sat on an element. Bread tumbled from a plastic bag, scattering crumbs across the countertop. A block of cheddar cheese on a cutting board had a dirty knife beside it. She thought of Ben's super-neat kitchen and decided this Adele person must be as messy as Dad.

"I'm not hungry," she said coldly.

"I can make some," Katie said. "I'm starving!"

Sheila glared at her. She did a lot of glaring these days.

When Katie handed her a golden brown, toasted sandwich with melted cheese oozing onto the plate, Sheila couldn't help it. She took a bite. It tasted amazing. She took another bite and stared outside at the garden, trying to ignore Katie, who was chatting with Adele as if they were old buddies.

Couldn't Katie figure out she wanted nothing to do with this *Adele?* Wasn't it bad enough this awful woman was sitting in her dad's kitchen, helping herself to food as if she owned the place? Sheila glared daggers at Katie, but her friend chattered on like an idiot. Didn't even glance Sheila's way. As much as she tried not to listen, Sheila heard Katie tell about the police visit this morning, the rifle in the truck and the fire at the development.

Adele wasn't smiling anymore. "But that's terrible!" she said. "Who would do such a thing?"

"Someone who has motive," Sheila grumbled.

Adele turned to her in surprise, her round pink mouth slid into a grim line. "No one has more motive than I do."

"What motive?" Katie asked.

"Glenmar Developers took advantage of my parents when Mom was so ill. My mother has Alzheimer's disease, which means she's lost most of her memory—she doesn't even know who I am anymore!" Adele paused. "Dad couldn't leave her alone and he couldn't afford to hire a companion for her while he was out working on the ranch, so he was forced to sell that piece of land to raise some money."

"But I thought your dad died!" Sheila said. She was trying very hard not to feel sorry for Adele, but she couldn't help thinking how terrible it would be if her own mom didn't recognize her.

Adele nodded, and her eyes went all teary. "Dad was stressed out, worried about Mom, worried about the ranch—you may know that Alberta ranchers have suffered a lot of setbacks in the last few years, what with climate change and that case of mad cow disease."

Sheila nodded. Katie scribbled in her notebook.

"Dad saw all their dreams fall apart. Even worse,

his life partner of almost fifty years couldn't remember who he was, much less the plans they had made together. Before she got so ill they were working with the Nature Conservancy of Canada to preserve the land. If only he had called me!" Adele stood up, walked to the counter and grabbed a tissue. "But he didn't, and then he had a sudden heart attack and..." Her voice trailed off as tears spilled down her cheeks.

Sheila tried to hang onto her anger at this woman who wanted to steal her father away, but it wasn't easy. "It's not your fault," she said.

Without looking up from her writing, Katie said, "But I still don't understand why you have a motive for setting fire to the development. I mean, they just have that little chunk of property where you can't even see them from your house. And they might not be very nice people, but if they paid for the land, it isn't their fault your dad was stressed out. They actually helped him by giving him money."

"Katie!" Sheila said. "Can't you stop asking questions for one minute? Mr. Arnesen was a really nice man and I liked him. I liked Mrs. Arnesen too."

Katie looked up, surprised. Then she saw Adele blowing her nose, tears rolling down her cheeks. "Oh!" she said. "I'm sorry!"

Adele swallowed and tried to smile. "Don't worry about it. You're right, really. Revenge isn't a good motive and I'm not that type of person. No, my problem is with Glenmar trying to take over the rest of my parents' land to build a golf course and housing and even a shopping mall! That couldn't be further from what my parents wanted—an environmental preserve for animals like the grizzly sow who uses both our ranches as part of her range."

"Have you seen her? Does she have cubs this year?" Sheila asked, excited to hear news of the mother bear she had seen several times in the distance, once with two tiny brown cubs.

Adele shook her head sadly. "No one has seen her this year."

Just then three bedraggled figures appeared at the door, their wet clothes clinging to their bodies.

"Mom! I didn't know you were coming home today!"

Mother and son hugged, briefly, before Adele pulled away. "You're soaking wet!" she laughed. "Get away from me!"

Sheila's dad gave her a quick kiss on the lips. "I didn't expect you back so soon!"

Adele sighed and winked at Sheila. "Here's a man who showed up late for class almost every day back in high school. Has he ever learned to keep track of time?"

Sheila shook her head. "Not as long as I've known him!"

14

After lunch, Huntley gathered up his things and tossed them in the back of his mom's car. He saddled his horse, put a bridle on his mother's horse and prepared to ride across the fields with both horses while his mom drove her car around.

Sheila stood beside her dad. She was happy they were going. Maybe now she could have her father to herself, if she didn't count Katie and Rusty.

Adele opened her car door. "Are you sure you didn't forget anything?" she called to Huntley.

"No," he grinned down from the saddle, "but I'll probably be over every day anyhow."

Sheila was surprised that this didn't bother her at all. Two days ago she wanted Huntley out of her sight forever, but he wasn't so bad, just so long as he didn't *live* here.

When her mom phoned that evening, Sheila was tempted to tell her everything. Maybe Mom could help. But then she remembered her promise not to get involved in anything close to a mystery, no matter what Katie did. After all, the main reason Mom sent Sheila off for the summer was to keep her out of trouble.

Mom had really freaked out that first week of summer vacation when she roared up to a crime scene in her police car and found Sheila and her friends there. But Sheila was pretty freaked out herself when they got kidnapped. Scary stuff. But that's what you get for having a friend like Katie. *Katie Reid, Private Investigator,* she called herself, even if no one but Sheila and Rusty knew it.

So Sheila made up her mind to say nothing. She couldn't take the chance Mom would make her come home. Not now, not when her dad needed help.

"How's your father?" Mom asked.

"He's...okay."

"Sheila, is something wrong?"

Yes! Everything! "No."

There was a long pause at the other end of the line.

Mom, Dad's in big trouble, and maybe you can help! The words rang so loud in her head that, for one frightening second, Sheila thought she had said them out loud.

"Sheila, your dad told me he has a girlfriend. I remember meeting Adele once, before you were born. I liked her. So if that's what you're afraid of telling me..."

"You knew?"

"Not until tonight. Your dad and I talked before he called you to the phone. I told him I'm happy for him. I'm sure Adele is much more suited to ranch life than I ever was."

A heaviness settled way down deep in Sheila's stomach. Later she would think over her mother's words and wish things could have been different, but right now there were even more important matters to deal with. "Did he tell you anything else?"

Another pause. "Like what?"

Like everything's falling apart around here! Dad might be arrested! He might lose the ranch! But maybe Mom didn't care. "Like, Adele has a son named Huntley."

"Yes. He mentioned that too. He says the four of you are getting along well. So do you like Huntley?"

"I guess."

"Good. I'm glad you're having a great time even if I miss you so much. It's lonely around here without you, Sheila."

"I miss you too, Mom."

"So I'll talk to you soon then. I've got to get ready for work now, I'm on night shift."

"Bye, Mom."

"Bye, honey."

And that was that. Sheila slowly hung up the phone. Her mom didn't even ask after Silver or her own horse, Ingot. Sheila had always assumed Mom missed the ranch as much as she herself did. It seemed like she was wrong.

Sheila remained seated in her dad's office, where it was quiet and she could be alone. If she was so wrong about her mom, maybe she was wrong about her dad too. Maybe she didn't know either of them like she thought she did.

She got up from the desk and walked over to the closet. She tried the door. It wasn't locked and she pulled it open. Inside, the gun-cabinet door was unlocked too, but of course there were no guns there now. The RCMP had carted them away.

She stared at the two empty spaces. If her dad had taken a rifle and driven out to shoot the night watchman, why wouldn't he have put the rifle away when he got back? He might be careless about times and dates and be a bit disorganized and messy, but he would never leave a dangerous weapon lying around in his truck. Of that, Sheila was positive.

When Sheila left the office she still didn't feel like talking to anyone. At home, with just her and Mom around, she was used to having lots of time to herself. But since being on this vacation, she barely got a moment alone, and sometimes all those people, all those voices, made her want to scream. She needed quiet. She needed time to think.

Sheila walked through the kitchen and into the hall. The sound of a movie came from the living room. She wanted to walk right on by, go up to her room and close the door. But if she did that, someone would be sure to come looking for her, so she stopped at the entrance. "I'm tired," she said. "I'm going to bed."

Neither Katie nor Rusty bothered to answer; their eyes were glued to the TV. "Goodnight, Sheila," her dad said and turned back to the video.

Must have been a good movie.

Again the next morning, Sheila woke up early. She lay in bed watching shadows on the ceiling and trying to remember why she felt that sad, sinking feeling in her stomach. Was it because her mom didn't like the ranch anymore, or maybe never did? Was it because Mom didn't even care if Dad had a girlfriend? Yes. It was those two things and more. Something even worse. Then it came to her. Dad was in big trouble and she had a feeling something really terrible was about to happen. Today.

She slid out of bed, grabbed a bundle of clothes and tiptoed from the room. She would dress in the bathroom. That way there was no danger Katie would suddenly open one eye, groan and ask why Sheila was getting up so early.

Maybe, she thought as she pulled on her jeans and T-shirt, if her dad was up, they could go for a ride together.

Just as she had hoped, she found her dad in the kitchen, drinking coffee. His elbows rested on the table, his chin in his hands, and he stared outside, deep in thought. At the sound of her footstep he turned. "Good morning!" he said, making a brave attempt to smile. His blue eyes were red-rimmed and had dark circles around them, his sandy-colored hair stuck out from his head like tumbleweed, and he had a dark, stubbly beard.

Sheila wondered if he had slept at all the night before, but she couldn't find the words to ask him. Her dad was a man of few words, and he didn't like to be pestered with questions. Over the years, Sheila had learned to be patient, to wait for him to tell her what was on his mind, never to ask directly.

So she opened the fridge door, found a fat, juicy peach and grabbed a banana from the bowl on the counter. She sat down to join him.

"You're up early," he said.

Sheila nodded. "I thought maybe we could go for a ride before Katie and Rusty get up?"

He looked at her banana, reached his long arm over the counter and grabbed one for himself. He peeled it and was about to take a bite when he seemed to change his mind. "I need to ride out and talk to Wendell. You can come along if you like."

"Sure, Dad."

"I want to find out if he saw anything on the night of the fire. Maybe he can help me figure out what's going on around here."

"He says he saw you when the night watchman was shot."

"I know. I can't understand why he would say that."

"He saw your black hat and white feather."

Dad shook his head. "Couldn't have. I was wearing it and I was nowhere near the development." He bit into the banana and stood up.

Sheila left a note for Katie and Rusty, just in case they came downstairs before she and her dad got back from their ride.

They were in the barn saddling their horses when they heard the crunch of wheels on gravel. Dad walked outside and Sheila followed at a distance.

For a second Sheila thought the white SUV that pulled into the yard was Adele's. Then she wished it was. Instead, it belonged to the RCMP.

15

The doors opened and the same two RCMP officers stepped out: the thin, wiry one from the passenger side; the big, chunky one from behind the wheel. They didn't see Sheila and her dad and started toward the house.

"Can I help you gentlemen?" Dad called, walking into the farmyard. Sheila remained where she was.

The Mounties both swung around. The big one's hand hovered near the gun clipped to his belt. When they saw who it was, they relaxed slightly, but their expressions were glum. Sheila slunk back into the shadows.

The big one spoke first. "We need to ask you some questions."

"Anything I can do to help," her dad said politely. "Shall we go inside? There's coffee..."

"I'm afraid we'll need you to come with us," the thin man interrupted.

"But I don't understand."

"We're taking you in for questioning. You may need to stay for some time."

"That's impossible! I can't leave the ranch...and I have three children here. I can't abandon them."

"I'm afraid you have no choice," the Mountie told him. "Is there someone you can call?"

"Are you saying I'm under arrest?"

Sheila felt like running at the two men. She wanted to scream that her father was innocent. *Get out of here and go find out who really did it!* But she simply stood, still as stone, in the shadow of the barn door and watched and listened.

"You haven't been charged with anything."

"Then..."

"The bullet that shot the night watchman came from one of your rifles," the big officer told him. "And both rifles have been fired recently."

Her father sagged. For a second, Sheila thought he would fall and she was about to run to him, but he straightened and started for the house. "I don't know how that can be," he said, "but I'm sure we can straighten it out." Suddenly he seemed to brighten. "What about fingerprints? Did you check for prints?"

"Both rifles contained multiple sets of prints."

Her dad quickened his pace. "I need to call Adele James. As soon as she arrives to be with the kids, I'll come with you."

Sheila stood alone in the shadows while the two officers walked on either side of her father toward that hateful red door.

While the men were in her dad's office, Sheila ran upstairs. She burst into her room and pounced on Katie. "Wake up!" she said, shaking the limp form under the covers. "Katie! Wake up!"

"Wha..." Dark tousled curls and startled brown eyes appeared above the crumpled sheet. "What's going on? Why'd you wake me up? What time is it?"

Sheila sat on the edge of the bed and stared at her best friend. She tried, but no words would come out of her mouth.

Katie sat up, rubbing her eyes. "Sheila! What's wrong?"

"Katie, you've got to do something! They're arresting him!"

"What? Your dad? Why?"

"They said a bullet from his gun shot the night watchman."

Katie leapt out of bed and scouted around for

some clothes. First she looked under the bed, then she lifted the covers. Then she stood in the middle of the room in her pajamas with her hands on her hips. She spotted her clothes draped over a chair and ran over to grab them. "That's no big surprise," she said.

"Katie! How can you say that?"

"It's true. I mean, one of the rifles was missing, right? Your dad said he didn't know where it was and neither did Ben. So if they're both telling the truth, then someone must have stolen it on the night in question. Why would anyone bother to take it if they weren't going to use it?"

"But how? You said the locks hadn't been tampered with. And how did it get into my dad's truck?" An odd feeling came over Sheila, a sense that she knew something without quite knowing what it was. *You might know something you don't know you know.*

Katie was dressed by then and picked up a brush to run over her short curly hair. "Someone else may have a set of keys. What about Adele? Maybe she borrowed your dad's keys and had copies made."

Sheila thought of Adele showing up when no one was around, sitting in the kitchen as if she owned it. "But Adele was in Calgary."

Katie shrugged. "So she says."

"She's my dad's girlfriend, they *like* each other. Why would she want to make him look guilty?"

"To cover her own tracks," Katie said matter-of-factly. "Maybe she's not really his girlfriend at all, maybe she's just pretending so she can set him up. Even Adele admitted she has the best motive."

"But..."

"What?"

"Adele's coming to stay with us until Dad gets back."

"Good." Katie walked to the door and pulled it open. "That way we can keep an eye on her. Whatever you do, don't let her think we're on to her."

Before going downstairs, they knocked on the guest-room door, where Rusty was sleeping.

"What?" a sleepy voice growled.

"Get up and come downstairs," Katie called through the closed door. "The police are here and Huntley's coming over."

Adele and Huntley arrived at the front door just as Rusty stumbled, bleary-eyed, down the stairs. Katie and Sheila met all three of them in the front hall.

Sheila studied Adele's face. The woman looked pale and shaken, and she rubbed her hands together nervously. Sheila's eyes were drawn to the car keys that dangled from one finger on a key ring. There were a lot of keys.

She felt an elbow in her ribs and turned to see Katie frowning at her. Katie's eyes rolled to Adele in a meaningful way. She was trying to tell her something, but Sheila had no idea what.

"Sheila's brain isn't awake yet," Katie told Adele. She turned back to Sheila. "Adele asked where your dad is."

"Oh!" Now that was really weird. Scary too, because Sheila hadn't heard a thing. "I guess he's still in his office with those two, uh, men."

"You kids come on down to the kitchen. I'm going to tell them I'm here."

So who made you the boss all of a sudden? Sheila glared at Adele's ponytail as it swung down the hall.

Adele tapped once on the office door, then disappeared inside. Sheila, Katie, Rusty and Huntley waited in the kitchen, clustered together at the end of the counter, staring silently down the empty hall. It seemed like forever before the door opened again and Adele walked out, clinging to Chris's arm, her face tight and frightened. The RCMP officers followed close behind.

Sheila's dad stopped when he saw her. "Sheila," he said.

It seemed to her that his entire body slumped, like a rag doll, and she had never seen him look so sad. She ran over to him.

Dad pulled away from Adele and wrapped his arms around Sheila. "I'm so sorry you had to see this happen." He stepped back and looked down into her eyes. "But don't worry. I'm innocent, so everything will be okay. I may even be back by tonight." He kissed the top of her head. "I love you, girl. Promise me you'll stay right here, in the kitchen, until we're gone?"

Sheila nodded, unable to speak.

Her dad looked over at Huntley and attempted a smile. "Sorry to run off like this, Hunt, but I'll be back before you know it."

"Katie, Rusty," his sad eyes turned in their direction, "I suggest you try leaving a message on your grandparents' cell phone; maybe they can come pick you up. You too, Sheila, if you want to go..."

"I'm staying," she said fiercely.

"It's time." The big officer took her dad by the arm and led him toward the front door. Sheila turned away. She clutched the countertop to keep from running after him.

When the front door closed behind them, Sheila

glanced at Adele, half expecting to see a victorious smile spread across her face. But the woman looked anything but happy. She trembled with anger. "They'll pay for this!" she said, fists clenched at her sides.

"Who?" Sheila asked.

"Those goons at Glenmar!" Adele crossed her arms, cupping her elbows in her hands, and proceeded to pace back and forth across the kitchen, staring at the floor.

Sheila caught Katie's eye. So Adele had a temper. Interesting.

Adele poured herself a coffee and marched into Chris's office, leaving the door wide open behind her. They soon heard her talking on the phone, so quietly they couldn't tell what she was saying. If only she had closed the door they could creep down the hall and listen.

They barely spoke as they ate cereal, peaches and toast and peanut butter. Then Katie said, "We're staying too. Even if we could reach Gram and GJ, this is where we're needed."

"I'm going to call Mom," Sheila said. "Maybe she'll know what to do."

Katie nodded. "We'll wait outside," she said.

Sheila dialed her home and listened to the phone ring. She hung up when the answering machine clicked on. What could she say? She ran outside to join the other three.

Sheila really wished Huntley would go away, but for a completely different reason now than a few days ago. How were they supposed to keep an eye on his mother with him hanging around every minute?

They couldn't tell him what they suspected because he would probably go right to his mom and tell her everything. Even if he didn't tell her, he'd be angry.

Still, there was something Sheila had to do, and she realized it didn't really matter if Huntley came along or not. She hoped Katie would, though, sore butt or not. "I need to see Wendell Wedman," she said.

"Why?" Katie asked.

"That's where Dad and I were going when the RCMP showed up. He wanted to ask Wendell if he saw anything the night of the fire. And he was going to ask exactly what Wendell saw on," her eyes rolled to Katie, "the *night in question.*"

"Oh," Katie replied without enthusiasm, "so you're going to *ride* all the way out there?"

Sheila nodded. "It would take us forever to walk."

"Good idea," Huntley said, already on his way to the barn. "Let's get the horses saddled. Can I ride Ingot?"

Sheila nodded absently. She turned to Katie. *Please!* she silently begged. Her friend's face was a mix of interest and dread. "You've had a day off from riding," Sheila said. "You should be okay now."

Katie looked doubtful, but she glanced toward the open barn door and down at the notebook tucked under her arm. She tapped the cover with her fingertips. "Okay, but we just go straight there and straight back, no side trips, okay?"

Sheila nodded. "It's a promise."

They both turned to Rusty. He rolled his eyes, rubbed his backside and said, "What's a little more pain in my life? Pain is my middle name."

"I thought it was Jerold," Katie said, "after Grandpa Jerry."

"That too. But I'm adding *Pain* because it suits my lifestyle."

Sheila would have laughed if she didn't feel so sick with worry.

16

The damage was clear from the hillock above Glenmar Development. The portable closest to the barbed wire fence was nothing more than a rectangle of blackened, twisted metal. One side of the second portable was also black, some of the metal had buckled, and the window glass had blown completely out of its frame. The lower branches of the nearby pines were singed and brown, and the grass in between looked black as tar.

The backhoe, bulldozer and SUV, all parked near the edge of the reservoir, looked to be undamaged. Not far from them, under a copse of cottonwoods, was a large travel trailer.

"It's lucky the fire didn't spread through those pine trees," Sheila observed.

Huntley agreed. "Mom says it's a good thing we had

lots of rain last week or those trees would have gone up like torches and taken out most of the forest on our property too. But anyway, she heard on the news that the owners happened to stay here last night, so they managed to douse the flames before they spread."

"What a lucky coincidence," Katie murmured. "And isn't it fortunate they moved the machines and SUV before the fire?"

"Hey there, kids!" a voice called. "C'mon down!" A dog started barking behind them.

Wendell Wedman was standing down near the stream. He waved, then turned away to quiet Rebel.

They hobbled the horses to graze on the hillside and walked down to the stream. By then Rebel was wading in the shallows, scouting for interesting rocks. Wearing high rubber boots, Wendell stood in the middle of the stream, holding a large water keg. Two more kegs just like it stood on the gravel shore. He removed the lid, laid the keg in the water facing upstream and let it fill.

Sheila remembered swimming here with her mom, but now the water was so low it wouldn't reach her knees. Dad must be angry at Glenmar Development for diverting the stream like that. He needed the water for his fields and cattle. Her thoughts shifted to the trumpeter swans. This was their nesting period, but there wasn't enough water for them anymore. Everything was being ruined by that stupid development.

When the keg was full, Wendell replaced the lid, screwed it tight, picked up the keg by its wide, sturdy handle and made his way carefully over slippery rocks to shore.

He placed the heavy keg beside the other two. "Well, that's done," he said.

This time Katie had brought her notebook stuffed in her backpack. She got it out now and opened it.

"You got more questions?" he asked warily.

"Um, a few. Sheila does too."

"In that case, you kids better make yourselves useful." He picked up the keg with one wiry arm and started to trudge up the slope toward his van. "Think you can carry those other two kegs for me?"

"Simple!" Rusty ran over to one of them. He grabbed the handle, pulled, strained and managed to move the keg about one centimeter off the ground. He struggled forward one full step and put it down again.

"Want some help?" Huntley asked. With both boys clutching the handle, they managed to lift the heavy keg high enough to lurch forward with it.

The girls walked over to carry the third keg. Sheila was surprised by how heavy it was, even with Katie's help. Wendell must be stronger than he looked. The girls didn't do much better than the boys, but arrived at the van slightly ahead of them. Wendell had already finished emptying the first keg into the van's water tank.

He turned, took the girls' keg from them and lifted it to pour the water into a funnel he had rigged up on his water intake pipe. He watched Rusty and Huntley struggle up the last of the slope. "Simple, eh?" He winked at Rusty.

Red-faced and puffing, Rusty put down his side of the keg, straightened up and rubbed his hand. There was a bright red mark across it where he had gripped the handle. He grinned. "Easy for you to say."

Wendell refused to answer any questions until he had emptied every drop of water into the tank. Then he muttered something about the kettle and disappeared inside his van.

The boys wandered back down to the stream and tossed sticks for Rebel. Katie waited with Sheila. They sat on rickety folding chairs beside a lopsided card table covered with a red and white plastic tablecloth. Katie read her notes. Sheila tapped her foot impatiently. She thought of taking out her new Discman, which could play music through either speakers or headphones. Music would help soothe her jangled nerves, but what if Katie insisted on listening too? She left it in her backpack.

When Wendell returned, he was carrying a metal tray with five mugs and a plate of chocolate cookies. He carefully placed it on the table and lowered himself onto a folding chair. "Hope you like tea," he said. "Help yourselves."

The boys must have smelled food because they both appeared within seconds and each snatched up a couple of cookies. Rebel charged up the slope and darted around like a maniac, flinging water on everyone. But when the boys took their mugs and settled on the grass, the dog perched in front of them, his long, pink tongue hanging out.

Katie took this opportunity to ask her first question. "When the night watchman was shot, where did you say the truck was parked?"

"Far as I recall, I didn't say."

"Well then, where was it parked?"

"Seems like it went down there first." Wendell nodded toward the spot where the girls had earlier noticed tire tracks. "Looks to me like it ended up in the wrong place. Anyway, it stopped and turned around there, then zipped over the ridge. Didn't hear a thing, and that stupid mutt never made a peep. Mind you, I didn't see the truck down there, just the tracks it left behind."

"So did you ever see the truck?"

"Yep. After I heard the shots and ran outside."

"But you said it was on the other side of the hill by then."

"Yep."

"So how did you see it?"

"Didn't. I heard it start up though, poppin' and growlin' and complainin' like it does. Finally spotted it over there." He pointed to a line of pines at the far end of the ridge. "Just before it disappeared into the trees."

"And you could tell what color it was? Even in the shadow of the trees?"

"Nope." He popped a whole cookie into his mouth and chewed noisily.

"Okay, then, how do you know it was blue?"

He finished chewing, swallowed and took a swig of tea. "Never said it was. Said I couldn't say for sure."

"But when we saw Huntley that day, he said the police were looking for a blue truck."

"True enough. That's what the night watchman told me when I went down to see him. It was me made the 911 call with that cell phone your dad insisted on lendin' me. Soon as I heard the sirens I hightailed it back home. Anyway, I'm guessin' he told the cops what he knew about the truck."

While Katie wrote in her notebook, Sheila realized it was her chance to ask a question, yet she hesitated, almost afraid of the answer. Now or never. She took a deep breath and plunged in. "Wendell, did you see my dad's truck two nights ago, before the fire?"

"Hmm, can't say as I did."

"So you didn't?"

"Saw a truck takin' off, same as before, over by those pines."

"Did you see anything else?"

"Can't say as I did, and I was sittin' right here too. Happen I couldn't sleep that night, it was hot as an oven in my van. Anyway, 'bout one thirty I wandered outside where it was cooler. Always did love watching the stars spinnin' around up there in the night sky. A silence, pure as peace, generally settles in 'round that time of night too."

"Generally?" Katie glanced up from her notes. "You mean it was different that night?"

"Sure was. All those voices natterin' away, how's a man supposed to relax?"

"What voices?"

"Couple of men, one woman. Voices carry a long ways on a still night, almost like over water."

"So you could hear what they said?"

"Can't say as I could. Only voices. Anyway, pretty

soon that truck scooted off, and then the sky lit up with fire. I climbed up the hill and saw those two Coutts standin' there, watchin' the fire like they'd lost the power to move."

"Then what?"

"Well, I ran back to my van, grabbed my fire extinguisher and charged over the hill yellin' my head off for them to meet me at the fence."

"And?"

"That got them moving all right. The woman came runnin' over, surprised as anything and none too pleased judging by the look on her kisser. She snatched the extinguisher and started sprayin' the second portable. Had to back off, though, 'cause the fire was too hot. The man started up a hose and went after the fire spreadin' across the grass. Managed to put it out before the trees went up."

"That was lucky," Sheila said.

"Sure was. Anyway, guess they called the cops after that, don't know for sure. There was nothin' more I could do. I went back to bed and slept like a rock until after the sun came up."

17

Riding back home, Sheila almost dared to believe her dad would be there when they got back and that everything would be all right. But of course it wasn't.

Adele's little white SUV was still parked in the same spot, but now a small black Jeep with no roof was parked beside it. "That's Ryan's," Huntley said.

They found Ryan inside the barn, mucking out stalls and not looking happy about it.

"Hey, Ryan!" Huntley called. "When did you get back?"

Ryan removed the cigarette that dangled between his lips. "Late last night."

"Did you hear about the fire?"

"Yeah, Dad told me." He turned to Sheila. "I heard your dad's been arrested. Tough luck, kid." He patted her on the shoulder as if she was his pet dog or something.

Sheila backed away. "He wasn't arrested! The Mounties took him in for questioning." She was about to tell Ryan not to call her "kid," but when she looked down at the cigarette held between his fingers, with a glowing line of ash drooping from it, she said instead, "You're not supposed to smoke in the barn. With all this hay around, you could start a fire. You know better than that."

Anger flashed in his eyes; then he nodded. "You're right, kid, sorry." He went outside and stomped the cigarette into the dirt. When he returned, Katie had her notebook and pen at the ready.

"What are you doing?" Ryan growled. "Taking note of my bad behavior?"

"Katie writes notes about everything," Sheila explained.

"It's because she has a rotten memory," Rusty added.

Katie managed to include them all in her angry glare. She snapped the notebook shut. "Did you go to the Calgary Stampede?" she asked.

He looked surprised. "I have no interest in rodeos. Why would I go to the stampede?"

Katie shrugged. "I thought your dad said you went there."

Ryan shook his head. "He might have told you I went to Calgary to see my girlfriend. We went out for dinner and to a movie. If I never see another horse or cow after I'm done here this summer, I'll be a happy man."

"But I thought you liked the ranch!" Sheila said.

"Sure, it wasn't bad—when I was a kid. I've got better things to do now."

His words hurt Sheila, and she turned her back on him. She busied herself showing Katie how to remove the saddle and bridle.

Ryan muttered something about repairing a fence and rode off in his Jeep.

"He always uses the Jeep now," Huntley said, "so he doesn't need to ride a horse. Last year he used to like it here. Now he criticizes everything."

"Weird," Sheila said. She remembered how Ryan used to complain at the end of every summer when he had to return to his mom's place in Lethbridge. He loved the ranch then. What had changed? "Why'd he come here if he doesn't like it?"

"Who knows? I guess he needs the money for university. He wants to be a lawyer, you know."

Okay, maybe that explained it, Sheila decided. Maybe going to university makes people think they're way special. "What's his girlfriend like?"

"I don't know. She's never been here because she never wants to leave Calgary. Ben says she's real old, like maybe twenty-three."

Twenty-three! Sheila couldn't imagine ever being so old.

Outside, Rusty had settled in a plastic chair under the cottonwoods with his sketchbook propped on his knees. Katie began to search the dusty yard, her nose close to the ground and a little plastic bag in her hand.

"What are you looking for now?" Sheila asked.

Katie waved the bag. "Evidence!"

Curled inside the bag was a little brown and white object that resembled a caterpillar. Sheila realized what it was: a long cigarette butt.

"Where'd you get that?"

"By the door. It's the one Ryan dropped."

Sheila remembered the cigarette butts up on the hill above the development and felt a little burst of hope. "So do you think it was Ryan?"

"Don't know yet. Could be."

"Why did you ask if he went to the stampede?"

"I just wanted to know if he was in Calgary or not."

"Why?"

"Because that's where the matches were from, remember? A restaurant in Calgary."

"But Ryan was away when the fire started, and Adele was here. She was in Calgary a few days ago though. Maybe the matches were hers."

"Hmm, can't say as I know." Katie grinned.

"We need to talk to Adele," Sheila said.

They found her at the desk in Chris's office, reading a letter. Adele looked up, bleary-eyed, as Sheila and Katie entered the room.

"Lawyer babble," she said, shaking her head. "Why can't they write in plain English so people can make sense of it?"

Katie shrugged. "Maybe they're trying to impress everyone with how smart they are."

"Like Ryan," Sheila said without thinking.

Adele and Katie laughed.

"What are you reading about?" Katie asked, trying to read upside down.

"It's from Glenmar Development's lawyers. They're saying Glenmar has the right to purchase the entire Cottonwood Creek ranch for their development scheme. Imagine, all that beautiful land paved over, filled with houses and a shopping mall! The idea makes me ill!"

"But how can they buy it if you don't want to sell?" Sheila was appalled. She had loved this land for as long as she could remember. The Waltons and the Arnesens had always kept their adjoining lands as natural as possible for the wild creatures that had lived here since long before settlers arrived.

"Apparently, after my parents sold that chunk of land to them, Glen and Marla Coutts kept pestering them to sell the rest of the property. Mom no longer understood what was happening, because of her disease." Adele shuddered and put her hand to her mouth. "But before Mom became ill, my parents had planned to preserve their land as a conservation easement."

"What's that?" Sheila asked.

"It's an arrangement they were making with the Nature Conservancy of Canada. The environmental value of the land would always be maintained, but our family would continue to own it. That way the natural habitat would be preserved for wildlife species forever."

What a great idea, Sheila thought, if only it had worked.

"I still don't get it," Katie said. "How can Glenmar get your land if you don't want to sell it?"

"My dad was still making arrangements with the Nature Conservancy when he died so suddenly. It looks like the Couttses zipped right over and got my mother to sign over her land, even though she had no idea what she was signing."

"But—that's disgusting!" Sheila said. She couldn't imagine anyone sneaking around like that, taking advantage of someone with a horrible illness like the one Mrs. Arnesen had.

"Your dad has been helping me," Adele said, "and he wants to do the same thing with the Triple W ranch. What we'd really like to do is start a guest ranch and ecological reserve where people can come to learn about nature. But, anyway, Chris is helping pay for a lawyer to defend our rights. My lawyer says Mom's signature isn't valid due to her condition." Suddenly Adele slammed both fists against the desk so hard that both girls jumped. "Everything's such a mess!" she shouted. "And now your dad's in trouble! How can we afford to hire another lawyer to help him?"

Sheila felt ill. It was so unfair! And she was suddenly certain Adele had nothing to do with the shooting or the fire, even though she did have a good motive. But if not Adele, then who? Who else had motive? Not Ryan. He couldn't get away from here fast enough.

That left her dad.

"Listen," Adele said, "I need to go back to my place this afternoon for a few hours. The boys are coming with me. Do you girls want to come along, or will you be okay here?"

"We'll be fine," Katie said.

18

"I've almost got it worked out," Katie said. She was sitting cross-legged on the grass under the cottonwood trees after Adele and the boys drove away.

On a lawn chair nearby, Sheila wiggled her bare toes and paid little attention. She listened absently to the steady *clink, clink, clink* of metal on metal from the far side of the barn and pictured Ben working away in the heat of his blacksmith shop, designing the perfect horseshoe for whichever horse needed re-shoeing at the moment. "Ben's a farrier, you know."

"Oh," Katie mumbled. Then she looked up. "What's a farrier?"

"He looks after horses' feet—not just our horses, but for all the ranchers in the area, and he makes shoes to fit them properly."

Katie shrugged and checked her notes. "There's only one thing that doesn't make sense."

Again Sheila paid no attention. She was locked in her own little world, trying to think things through. There was no getting around the fact that, even if Wendell didn't get a good look at it, the truck at the crime scene pretty much had to be her Dad's because it left the scene heading across Walton land, not by way of the new road built by Glenmar.

Also, even if she really wanted Adele to be guilty, there was no way anyone could confuse Adele with Dad, not even by moonlight. Adele was short and plump; Dad was tall and muscular. So if not Adele, who?

Her mind leaped to Wendell Wedman. What if Wendell made it all up? What if he did the shooting and started the fire himself, then made up a story about seeing the truck and her dad?

"What about Wendell?" she cried, excited.

Katie looked up and shook her head. "Nope! I thought of that, but it doesn't work."

"Why not?"

"How would he get the gun? And the truck was out there that night, we have evidence to prove it, so Wendell couldn't have made that part up. Besides, what motive does he have?"

Sheila had a sudden inspiration. "Maybe he's working for Glenmar Development. Maybe they paid him to lie about what he saw so they could get my dad out of the way. Maybe they did it to themselves with Wendell's help..." Her voice trailed off.

"You're on the right track," Katie said. "But that still doesn't put the rifle in his hands, or put him in the truck. I think I know who did it. I just need to figure out one thing that doesn't fit."

"What?"

"Your dad told me he didn't shoot his rifle when he was out on the north range, but you heard the police say both rifles had been fired. Why would your dad lie to me?"

"He didn't lie!" Sheila snapped. She thought back, trying to recall his exact words. Then she had it. "Dad never said he hadn't shot the rifle. He told you he didn't shoot at anything. Dad would never kill an animal unless it was absolutely necessary. He always fires in the air to scare predators away. He doesn't shoot *at* them."

"Hmm..." Katie chewed on the end of her pen and studied her notes. She flipped pages in her notebook, back and forth, back and forth. "Hmm," she said again.

Sheila couldn't stand it any longer. "What?" she shouted.

Katie glanced up, startled. "Okay. There are two things we need to do. Do you think if we rode..." Katie winced, "...if we rode out to the north range, we could find the bullets your dad fired?"

Sheila shook her head. "No way. Do you know how much land is out there? Covered in grass? The only person who might be able to find them is my dad; he knows where he was standing and which direction he fired. If we used a metal detector, maybe, but I don't know. Besides, even if we could, we can't. The police need to find the bullets themselves or they won't be any good as evidence. If we pick them up, how do we prove where we found them?"

"Good point," Katie said and made another note in her book.

"What's the other thing?"

Just then Ben appeared from the far side of the barn, his right arm cradled against his stomach as if it hurt. He saw the girls and called, "I hear you girls are on your own! Want to come down to the cottage for lunch?"

"Is it lunchtime already?" Sheila asked.

"What do you mean, *already*? I've been working in a sizzling hot shop all morning. I'm parched and my stomach is so empty it thinks my throat's been cut!"

Katie was already on her feet. "We'd love to have lunch with you!" she said with such eagerness that Sheila knew she had something other than food on her mind.

"Good, I'll see you there in a few minutes." He disappeared down the lane.

"That's the other thing!" Katie said. "We need to question Ben and talk to Ryan. I'll explain on the way."

They found Ben seated on a bench on his front porch, removing his boots. He took off his cowboy hat and wiped his damp brow with his left hand and, still using his left hand, took a drag on his cigarette and stubbed it out in a big ashtray. Sheila wrinkled her nose.

"Hi, Ben," she said, "want some help making lunch?"

"That'd sure be nice. I'm pooped! I was hoping Ryan would get back before me and have lunch ready. That's one thing he's still good at—he's a great cook." He stood and opened the door. "How do you kids feel about peanut butter and banana sandwiches? That's my specialty. Ryan used to like them too, but he turns his nose up at them now."

"Sounds scrumptious!" Sheila said and followed Ben inside.

Ben took an ice pack from the freezer and wrapped it around his elbow.

"I thought your sore elbow would be better by now." Sheila remembered how Ben's elbow bothered him the spring before she left the ranch. It got so bad he finally went to a doctor, who told him he had arthritis and shouldn't use it so much.

"It's not so bad," Ben said now, "if I'm careful." He made a pot of coffee and mixed two glasses of chocolate milk while Sheila spread peanut butter on multigrain bread and Katie sliced bananas on top.

"Ryan won't approve," Ben said as they carried their lunch to the table. "Not fancy enough for the likes of him. I don't know what's gotten into that boy lately—I have my suspicions though."

"University?" Sheila asked.

Ben shook his head. "Not so much university as the company he keeps in Calgary."

"You mean his girlfriend?" Sheila said.

"He hasn't been the same since he met Michelle. He seems nervous and angry all the time, and nothing anyone does around here is good enough for him. And you know? He won't be seen wearing a cowboy hat!"

"But I thought I saw him wearing a black one," Katie said.

"Black?" He looked surprised. "Not Ryan. He used to have a brown one, like mine, but not anymore."

"I need to use the bathroom," Katie said, pushing up suddenly from the table. As before, she gave Sheila a warning glance, but this time Sheila knew what Katie had in mind and shook her head. *No!*

Katie ignored her.

"You know where it is," Ben said. As soon as Katie was out of sight, he whispered, "Your friend must spend half her life in bathrooms!"

Sheila laughed nervously. "Not quite." She bit into her sandwich. Yum, nothing better. But she too had a question for Ben. "Don't you like Ryan's girlfriend?"

"Uh, let's say she wouldn't be my first choice. Michelle comes from a rich family. Seems like all Ryan thinks about now is money."

As Ben spoke, the front door flew open and in walked Ryan.

"Ryan!" Sheila shouted. She hopped off her chair so fast it crashed to the floor.

Ryan looked surprised and Ben gave her an odd look, but Sheila knew she had to do something, and quick. She was sure Katie was in Ryan's room right this minute, searching for—something. Whatever. She ran over, grabbed Ryan's wrist and tried to drag him through the living room toward the kitchen. "Come have lunch; we made your favorite!"

After a few steps Ryan pulled back. "What?" He sniffed the air. "Peanut butter and banana sandwiches? Oh, please! I haven't eaten one since I was a little kid like you!"

Sheila stifled the anger that flashed through her. "Try one, you might like it."

He laughed and shook his head. "I don't think so. I'll make something for myself after I get cleaned up." He turned and walked toward the hall.

Sheila heard a footstep. "Ryan!" she called.

He swung around. "What now?"

"How about some chocolate milk?" she grinned. Out of the corner of her eye, she saw Katie emerge from farther down the hall and pass by the bathroom. Katie didn't miss a step as she opened the bathroom door on her way past.

Ryan snorted. "Chocolate milk? I don't think so." He passed Katie on her way back to the kitchen. "Where did you come from?" he asked suspiciously.

Katie looked up with innocent brown eyes. "The bathroom." She rubbed her stomach. "I drank too much chocolate milk."

As she passed Sheila, she nodded almost imperceptibly.

The girls sat down again. Ben glanced back and forth between them, but his eyes widened when Katie raised her half-finished glass of chocolate milk. "Are you sure you should drink that?" he asked.

Katie nodded, her dark eyes wide over the rim of her glass.

"It's Wednesday today," Sheila pointed out in an effort to divert his attention.

Ben nodded.

"Do you still go to town every Wednesday afternoon for supplies?"

He nodded again. "I'm heading out right after lunch. Should be gone until after dark. I'm meeting a friend for dinner."

"A lady friend?" Sheila asked.

Ben grinned. "A friend," he repeated.

"We'll clean up the kitchen so you can get going," Katie offered. "We don't mind, do we, Sheila?"

Sheila shook her head. "Don't worry, we'll do an excellent job."

"That's real nice of you girls." Ben finished his coffee and took his mug to the sink. "You may as well wait until Ryan's done. He'll only mess things up again."

"We don't mind," Sheila said.

"We'll drink some more chocolate milk while we wait," Katie said.

Ben gave her a worried look, opened his mouth as if to say something, but quickly changed his mind. "I'll go and get cleaned up then. Thanks, kids. I'm running a bit late."

19

As soon as the door to Ben's room closed, Sheila turned to Katie.

"What happened?" she asked.

"I found a long white feather and a white hatband hidden in Ryan's underwear drawer," said Katie.

"Cool!" Sheila whispered, suddenly feeling more hopeful. "So what do we do now?"

Although Katie had outlined her plan, they hadn't known if they would get a chance to make it work. Everything depended on getting Ryan alone. Even so, now that Ben was heading to town, Sheila had misgivings. "Why don't we tell the police what we know?"

"Right. Do you think they'll listen to a couple of kids?" Katie shook her head. "No. We need to have good, solid evidence. A white feather and some cigarette butts won't do it."

"We have the matches too, from a restaurant in Calgary."

"Calgary's a big place. Anyone could have picked up matches there and dropped them above the development."

"So why do you think it's Ryan?"

"Um, I'm not sure—I could be wrong. It's either Ryan or—"

"Or who?"

"There's only one way to know for sure."

By the time Ben walked out the door and Ryan emerged from his room wearing clean clothes, the girls had rehearsed what they needed to say.

They remained at the table while Ryan chopped vegetables, heated a wok on the gas stove, added olive oil and tossed in the vegetables. He threw in some Chinese noodles and added cooking wine, soy sauce, sesame seeds and a few other things Sheila didn't even recognize. Both girls watched the growing mess on the countertop: cutting board, knives, spoons, little plates and bowls.

"I'm sure glad you guys offered to clean up," Ryan said as he settled on a stool by the counter with his back to them. He opened a book, propped it up on the counter and started to read.

Katie made a face at Sheila.

Sheila knew exactly what it meant. She felt the same way: Ryan thinks he's too good to sit at the table with us.

The girls began to speak in low tones to each other. Quiet, but loud enough for Ryan to hear easily.

"I can't wait till Dad gets home tonight!" Sheila said.

"Yeah," Katie agreed. "I'm glad Adele is arranging bail for him. When does he get back?"

"He'll probably be home by dinnertime. Adele's picking him up."

"I hope the police don't take him away again."

"Me too. Dad told the Mounties to question Wendell in case he saw something, but that won't help much. Some surefire help he turned out to be!"

"Who's Wendell?" Ryan asked, putting down his book and swinging around on the stool. "Not that old coot who camped over near Swan Pond last summer?"

"Didn't you know? My dad asked Wendell if he wanted to camp over near the development so he could keep an eye on it."

"I've never seen him!" Ryan narrowed his eyes suspiciously.

"Have you been over there this week?" Katie asked.

Ryan's eyebrows pulled together, he shrugged and looked away.

Katie persisted. "Because if you didn't go there, it's not too surprising that you didn't see him, is it?"

"Do you ever stop asking questions?" Ryan snarled and plunged his fork into his stir-fry.

"I guess the Mounties didn't know he was there either," Sheila said. "That's why they haven't questioned him yet. They only talked to the night watchman, and he identified the truck and my dad's cowboy hat. Wendell thinks the night watchman is lying."

"It's too bad Wendell didn't see anything," Katie added. "He feels bad about that."

"I thought he was supposed to be watching the place," Ryan said.

Sheila nodded. "That's why he feels so bad. Dad thought he'd be a surefire way of keeping Glenmar in check. But he slept through everything both nights. He's sure my dad is innocent, though, so he wants to be a witness."

Ryan pushed his plate away. "Who does he think did it?"

"He doesn't know, but he'd have to see it with his own eyes before he'd believe Dad had anything to do with it. So he plans to sleep outside every night, just in case whoever did it comes back. He was hoping something would happen while my dad was in police custody. That way Dad would have a perfect alibi."

Ryan left soon after that, leaving most of his meal untouched. "I've got work to do," he said. "Do a good job of cleaning up here. You know how fussy Dad is."

"Of course," Sheila said. "Are you going back to work on the fence?"

Ryan nodded. "I need to get that section fixed by tonight or my father will be on my case." He stomped out the door and slammed it behind him.

"Okay," Katie said. "We've got work to do." She looked unhappily at the dishes Ryan had used to mix his various concoctions, the wok with a slotted spoon sticking from it, vegetable peelings scattered around a plastic bucket, a bottle spilling soy sauce.

"After all that, he didn't even eat it!" Sheila said. "I think he was being as messy as possible just to make more work for us."

Katie sighed. "I'll take care of this. You need to ride out and warn Wendell something might happen tonight."

"Are you sure you don't want to come?"

Katie nodded. "You'll be way faster on your own. And I have to tell Huntley and Rusty as soon as they get back. Then we need to catch Ryan; we can't let him talk to Adele. He has to be absolutely convinced your dad is home tonight."

"I sure hope we're right about this!" Sheila said.

"One way or another, we should find out the truth tonight," Katie said.

It was late afternoon, and Sheila was back from seeing Wendell, when Adele's little white SUV rattled into the yard and parked beside the blue truck. Rusty and Huntley tumbled out of the backseat, each carrying a flat, square box. Adele climbed out, her arms loaded with paperwork. "I'm going to set up in your dad's office. I expect I'll be up half the night trying to make sense of all this gobbledygook," she flicked her fingers against the stack of papers, "so I guess I'll sleep in there tonight–if I manage to sleep at all."

"What about the frozen pizzas?" Huntley asked.

"First things first," Adele smiled. "Bring them inside and we'll put them in the oven. While the pizzas cook, can you kids see that the horses are fed and watered?"

"Sure," Sheila said.

"Good. Then I'll call you when dinner's ready."

When the boys joined them in the barn, Katie and Sheila told them everything that had happened while they were gone. "So it's important that Ryan believes Adele brought my dad home," Sheila finished.

Before the chores were completed, they heard Ryan's Jeep drive into the yard. They all went outside as it rolled slowly past the barn. "Hey, Ryan!" Katie called, waving. "Did you finish repairing the fence?"

He braked and switched off the engine. "What a job! I'm beat! How about you kids take care of the horses so I can go home and eat? I'm half starved!"

"You forgot to finish your lunch," Sheila reminded him. "I guess you were just so anxious to get back to work."

"Yeah, right." Ryan didn't get out of the Jeep, but he didn't seem in any hurry to leave either. His fingers tapped against the steering wheel. He glanced at Adele's white car and back to Sheila. "So? Did he make it home?"

"My dad?" Sheila smiled. "He sure did! I'm so happy! He doesn't feel very good though. He's had a real rough day so he went to bed already. Adele said she and Huntley will stay here tonight so Dad doesn't need to worry about anything."

"Yeah?"

Sheila nodded. "She brought loads of paperwork with her. She says she'll be awake most of the night anyway, so she may as well stay in Dad's office."

"Makes sense." Ryan turned the key to start the engine. "See you tomorrow. I've got to get an early night too." He continued past the barn, around the cottonwoods and along the narrow lane that led to Ben's cottage.

20

A huge, silvery moon floated high in a midnight-blue sky and painted the rolling grasslands with its pale and eerie light. Craggy mountains loomed high in the west like a giant castle wall, seeming closer at night than by day.

Sheila curled forward in the saddle. Her stomach ached so much she couldn't sit straight. She had never been so scared, despite the terrifying situations they had found themselves in this summer.

What if their careful plan didn't work? What if Ryan didn't show? If he didn't, then maybe, just maybe, her dad really was guilty. Even if he was innocent, he was in big trouble. As Katie always said, *Follow the evidence.* And the evidence pointed to her dad.

Sheila was glad she had decided to bring her CD

player along, clipped to her belt with the carrying pouch tucked safely in her backpack. She put the earphones on, turned the volume low and listened to her dad's favorite country CD. The familiar music helped keep her worries under control.

When they finally reached Wendell's van, he was waiting outside, his hand on Rebel's muzzle so he wouldn't bark. "You kids sure you want to get involved?" he asked. "I could likely handle this by myself. Might be better that way, one person can hide better than five."

"I need to be here," Sheila said. She dismounted and, clutching Silver's reins, turned to her friends. "You guys can go back if you want, I'll understand."

Katie shook her head. "You helped me before. I'm not deserting you now."

"I'm staying too," Huntley said. "Besides, what are friends for?"

Rusty cleared his throat uncertainly.

"Rusty, why don't you stay here in the van? No one blames you for being scared."

"Me? Scared? You bet your cowboy boots I am! But that never stopped me before. I do some of my best work when I'm scared out of my mind!"

They all laughed nervously.

"Let's get a move on then," Wendell said. "You've gotta get these horses out of sight."

They led their horses into the woods behind Wendell's van and tied them securely. Then they joined Wendell on his rickety folding chairs.

Wendell made some tea and brought out his chocolate cookies and some apples. For a while they nibbled on cookies, crunched apples, sipped tea and chatted nervously.

Time passed.

They finished all the food, drank all the tea and ran out of things to say. Rusty yawned first. Then Wendell. The night grew colder. And so quiet! The moon slowly moved across the sky. It was hanging, big and bold, above the mountains when Sheila heard a sound. Her ears perked up and she looked up toward the hill, a smooth, black silhouette in moon shadow. Did she hear a distant truck engine?

She sank back. No. It was Wendell, snoring softly, his chin resting on his chest.

Rusty was next to succumb. He rolled off his chair and curled on the grass. "Wake me up if anything happens," he mumbled. Then Huntley stretched out on his back with an arm across his eyes. Rebel settled happily between the two boys.

Katie yawned. Sheila couldn't help herself, she yawned too. And shivered. Her stomach hurt more than ever now. "Promise me you won't fall asleep?" she whispered.

"Don't worry." Katie yawned again.

Sheila's eyes drooped, her head sagged. She jerked awake. She needed to stand up, stretch, move around or she would fall asleep for sure. Katie must have felt the same way because she was on her feet before Sheila could summon the energy.

"Let's walk up the hill," Katie whispered. "Maybe we'll see something."

From the summit they gazed down at the development. The reservoir shone in silver moonlight. Beside it was a pale square of yellow light. "That's the trailer," Sheila whispered. "Maybe the Couttses are there. I wonder what time it is."

"Late," Katie said.

"I don't think he's coming."

Katie said nothing. Sheila's stomach twisted.

They continued down the slope to the barbed wire fence. That's when they heard it—an unmistakable clatter, the roar of an engine, frighteningly close. So close that when they turned to scramble back up the hillside, headlights were already bouncing over the lower branches of the pines.

"It's too late!" Katie said. "He'll see us!"

Sheila thought quickly. "We can follow the fence to the stream and circle around behind. We need to wake Wendell. He's our witness!"

They stumbled along in semi-darkness, following the fence line, but they hadn't gone far when the truck burst onto the hilltop. Headlights skimmed the alder branches above their heads.

"He's sure not trying to be quiet," Sheila said.

"Of course not. He *wants* Wendell to see him. He needs to make Wendell believe it's your dad up there, driving the blue truck and wearing the cowboy hat with the white feather."

"Get down!" Sheila warned.

The girls fell to the ground. Headlights carved an arc above their heads as the truck turned around. Its engine shut off. A door creaked open and slammed shut, followed by a quick *tick-tick-tick* and a poof of hot steam.

"If that doesn't wake up Wendell and the boys, then...Oh no!"

The night air was shattered by barking. Loud, excited barking, getting louder. Louder.

Sheila raised her head. A few steps below the hilltop, making its way toward the development against a background of moonlight, was the top of a dark hat and the tip of a white feather. It stopped. Turned around. Moved back up, fast, toward the truck.

Rebel's barks were even louder now, directly above. The truck door slammed shut. Rebel howled.

"Git back here you mangy mutt!" Wendell yelled, his voice distant. Rebel barked excitedly.

Sheila listened for the truck to start up. For it to drive away.

It didn't.

"Sit, Rebel! Sit!" Wendell was on the hilltop now, and at last Rebel stopped barking.

"You can get out now," Wendell shouted. "I'm holdin' Rebel back. Step out here and let me see your ugly face."

The door creaked open. "You!" Wendell shouted. "I don't believe it!"

"Me either!" a young voice said, and Sheila realized Huntley had joined Wendell.

Suddenly Rebel started barking again, a different bark now, deeper and mixed with a growl that came from deep in his chest. Barking, he charged down the hill toward the development.

"Call off your dog or I'll shoot him right here!" a man yelled from somewhere below.

"Rebel!" Wendell called. "Git back up here!"

Rebel kept barking.

"Don't shoot!" Wendell cried. "I'm comin' to get him!" A minute later he commanded, "Sit! Rebel, sit!" And Rebel was quiet.

"Put him in the truck!" the new voice ordered.

"And if I refuse?"

"You won't like the alternative."

"Do as he says," a woman's voice broke in. "No one needs to get hurt."

"C'mon, boy," Wendell grunted.

Sheila imagined him bending to take Rebel by the collar. The dog growled. "You two Coutts must have been lyin' in wait," Wendell said.

"You might say we've been expecting company," Glen Coutts said. "Hurry it up! We don't have all night."

The truck door opened. "In you go, boy," Wendell said. The door slammed shut.

"Good. Now what are we going to do with these two?" Glen asked.

"Bring them down to the portable. We'll decide from there." It was the woman who spoke.

"Must be Marla Coutts," Sheila whispered.

"Mmm," Katie agreed. "Shh!"

"Let the boy go," Wendell pleaded. "He's no harm to anyone. I promise to do whatever you say, just let him go."

The woman laughed. "To run and call for help? Do you think we're stupid?" Her voice turned harsh and angry. "Bring them both. That's Adele James' boy. You can be sure she'll promise anything to get her son home safely. It's too bad we didn't think of that in the first place."

Then a low voice broke in. The words were impossible to make out, but it sounded like a threat.

"You fool!" Marla said. "You're in this as deep as we are!"

The owner of the deeper voice responded, but the words were indecipherable. Sheila thought there was something familiar about the sound of the voice.

"Sorry, it's too late to change your mind, Cowboy. It wasn't us who shot the night watchman. But if you really want to join your friends here, fine. A scapegoat might come in handy."

"You heard the lady," Glen said. "Now get moving! All of you!"

21

"Rusty!" Katie dropped to her knees beside the sleeping form. He didn't stir. "Rusty!" She grabbed his shoulders and shook him.

"Wha..."

"Rusty, wake up! You missed everything."

"Huh?" he mumbled. "Where am I?"

"Lying on the grass in front of Wendell's van. Rusty, they've got Wendell and Huntley."

Rusty sat up and wrapped his arms around himself. "I'm cold." Suddenly, as if Katie's words finally sank in, he leapt to his feet. "Who's got them? Where? What happened?"

"It's those Glenmar people! The truck got here, but Rebel barked and woke everyone up. Wendell ran to stop him, but the Couttses must have heard the noise, and they showed up too. Glen Coutts has a gun! He made Wendell and Huntley go with them down to the portable."

"So did Ryan show?"

"Yes," Sheila told him. "I think so."

"What do you mean you think so? Either he did or he didn't."

"Okay, he did. But the Couttses have him too because I think he tried to protect Huntley and Wendell. Rusty, we've got to do something before it's too late."

Ten minutes later, Sheila, Katie and Rusty were hunkered below a small, lighted window of the portable. To their right were four wooden steps up to a tightly closed door.

"One of us needs to peek in," Sheila whispered.

"The tallest one," Katie suggested.

"And the most athletic," Rusty added.

"I guess we know who's elected," Sheila sighed.

Facing the wall, Sheila pressed her fingers against the cold aluminum, and dew dampened her hands. She straightened her knees and reached toward the sill above her head. Light poured out into the night. Her fingers curled around the thin aluminum sill and she pulled. The top of her head didn't quite reach the bottom of the window. She sank down again.

"I need something to stand on," she whispered.

Quickly and quietly, they scouted around the corner. Rusty pointed to a pile of clutter tossed from the burned portable. A metal chair lay on its side, almost intact. They placed it beneath the window.

Sheila climbed on the chair. Higher, higher, fingers on the sill, eyes level with the sill. An inch farther and she was looking inside.

A tall, slender woman with a thick mane of jet-black hair and a stocky man with dark blond hair stood close together, talking quietly, their backs to Sheila. The man, Glen, held a gun at his side.

The wall to Sheila's left was blackened and slightly buckled; not a shred of glass remained in the large window frame. But the remainder of the room looked surprisingly normal. In front of her were two desks and several office chairs, and beyond them was a large table holding what looked like a model of a small city: rows of little houses, a stretch of green grass with tiny flags at intervals like a miniature golf course, a pond and a cluster of larger buildings.

On the far side of the table, three people sat on straight wooden armchairs. But their arms didn't rest on the chairs. They were twisted behind their backs. Sheila couldn't see their feet, but guessed they must be tied. Behind them was another small window and a back door.

Wendell stared straight ahead, glaring daggers at the two Couttses. To his left was a younger man, but not as young as Ryan. He hung his head. Sheila wobbled and almost fell backward off the chair. She clutched the windowsill with her fingertips and stared in disbelief. Ben! Not Ben! How could it be Ben?

On Wendell's other side, Huntley stared right at her. He nodded almost imperceptibly, then his eyes shifted deliberately to Marla and Glen. They were walking toward the door. Sheila jumped off the chair.

"Get out of sight! Quick!" she whispered and led the way around the corner of the portable. Behind them the door was flung open so hard it smashed against the side of the building. Then it slammed shut again.

Sheila, Katie and Rusty pressed up against the wall and held their breath.

"This is just great!" Glen shouted. "How do you propose to get us out of this mess?"

"Obviously we can't let them go," Marla responded, her voice cool, composed.

"What do you want me to do? *Shoot them? The boy too?* How could you let this happen?"

"You went along quite happily until now, so don't blame me because some stupid old man and a nosy little kid got in the way."

"But no one was supposed to get hurt!" Glen moaned.

"Of course not. So what do you propose we do? Turn ourselves in?"

"And lose everything? Don't be stupid!"

"All right then," Marla said. "Obviously we can't shoot them. How would we explain that? But if that turncoat, Ben, were to show up here in the middle of the night to finish the job he started, then it will be his fault, not ours, if those two got themselves trapped inside a burning building. And if Ben accidentally got too close to the fire himself, no one would really be sorry, would they?"

"But how do we explain the boy and the old man being in there in the first place?"

"We don't. We know nothing about it. We weren't even here. Maybe Ben locked them inside because they caught him trying to set a fire."

There was a long pause. Sheila took shallow breaths. An acrid, burnt smell filled her nostrils and she realized she was pressed up against the blackened wall of the building.

"Believe me," Marla said, her voice softer now, "I wish there were another way."

"Me too," her husband replied, "me too."

The door opened and the couple went back inside.

Katie looked at Sheila and Rusty as they moved away from the grimy wall.

"Ben?" Katie whispered. "So it was Ben after all?"

"Yes, I can't believe it! I was sure it had to be Ryan!"

"Who *cares* whether it's Ben or Ryan in there?" Rusty danced from one foot to the other impatiently. "We've got to do something—now!"

"Right," Katie agreed. "Okay, let's think this through. Somehow we've got to lure the Couttses outside. But first, Sheila, tell us exactly what you saw in there."

After Sheila described the setup inside, they made their rescue plans.

22

"Are you sure you can handle this?" Sheila asked.

"Simple." Rusty's voice croaked with a fear he couldn't hide.

"No problem," Katie assured her, but she sounded as scared as Rusty. Katie fished her flashlight out of her backpack. "I'll keep this handy, we might need it."

The two set off for the barbed wire fence.

Sheila waited, listening, afraid the Couttses would make their move too soon. All alone, close beside the portable, Sheila clutched her CD player, tucked in its pouch with the headphones removed, tight against her stomach. The stink of singed metal and charred wood turned her stomach, but at least that horrible ache had gone away. Instead, she trembled with a deep, cold fear, and her heart beat fast against her ribs. Waiting was the worst part. Already it seemed like Katie and Rusty had been gone for hours.

If everything went exactly right, exactly as planned, they would all get out of this and no one would be hurt. She waited. And waited. Had something gone wrong? Then she heard barking up on the hill. She held her breath, her heart lurched. Almost time.

Please let everything go right!

She pictured Rusty up by the truck, holding Rebel's collar but encouraging him to bark like crazy. In a minute he and Katie would take Rebel down past Wendell's trailer. Sheila had told them exactly what to do, but could they handle it? Really?

If only Katie had stayed here and she had been the one to go...but they all agreed Sheila had the best chance of getting inside. And besides, she felt better with her friends out of danger. For the time being at least.

The door to the portable flew open. Heavy feet ran down the steps. "What on earth?" Glen shouted.

Marla's voice came from the porch. "That stupid dog has managed to escape! You must have left a window open. You'd better take care of it."

Sheila could see him then, his dark outline lumbering toward the barbed wire fence. Marla went back inside and closed the door.

It was time.

Sheila darted to the edge of the woods, about thirty feet from the portable. Beneath the pines, everything was black. She couldn't see. She placed a hand on the rough bark of the nearest tree, felt her way around it, walked a few steps farther in. And stopped. Listened. Silence. Good. Rebel had stopped barking. A good sign.

She glanced back at the lighted, glassless window, took a deep breath and placed her CD player on the ground behind the nearest tree. Ready. Now. She switched it on, full volume. Loud country music blared into the quiet night. Sheila ran for the portable.

The door burst open again as Sheila raced out of sight. Feet tumbled down the stairs. Sheila climbed onto the metal chair she had moved to the larger window. Her fingers curled over the frame and she boosted herself up and over. Almost. Half in, half out the window. Her legs stuck outside, waving frantically, and the top of her body hung inside the portable. With an expert flip she threw herself down, landed on her hands, tumbled over in a somersault and landed on her feet. Without breaking stride she ran to pull the door closed, locked it and raced toward three startled faces at the back of the room.

In a flash she had Huntley's hands untied. While he bent to untie his feet, she moved on to Wendell. But this knot was tight and she struggled with it. Meanwhile, Huntley freed himself and ran over to Ben.

"Leave him!" Sheila said. "Get out the back door! Quick, before Glen gets back with that gun!"

Before Huntley could reply, the music outside stopped abruptly. "Glen!" Marla screamed, her voice shrill as a siren outside the window. "Get back down here fast!"

"I can help you," Ben said quietly. "Please, Sheila, trust me. Do you think I would let them hurt you, Cowgirl?"

Cowgirl, how dare he call her that? Sheila's fingers fumbled with the knot.

"I believe him," Huntley said. "Ben feels real bad. He tried to help us already."

Sheila realized it would be better to have Ben's help than to leave him here, helpless. But if Huntley was wrong...

"Sheila?" Ben pleaded. "I'll do anything to make this up to you."

"Oh, all right! Just hurry!" The knot started to loosen. Almost. Almost. Yes! She pulled the rope free and crouched to help Wendell with the rope around his ankles.

Wham! Wham! Wham! Fists pounded against the front door.

"Let me in right now!" Marla screamed.

"Leave me!" Wendell said. "Take Huntley and get out the back while you still can."

The banging stopped. The rope came free. Sheila helped Wendell to his feet. Huntley had untied Ben's wrists, and Ben bent to free his ankles. "Run!" he said. "Now!"

"Hey!" Marla shouted, her face at the window. "Stop right there!"

Marla pulled herself up. Her head and shoulders were through the window, but she wasn't as agile as Sheila and dropped back out of sight. She tried again, clasped the sill, boosted herself higher until the top half of her body hung inside and she teetered on the narrow windowsill.

Sheila charged at her.

"No!" Marla screamed as Sheila pushed her back outside.

"Marla?" Glen called from the front of the portable. So close.

"Sheila!" Ben called. "Get out, now!"

She turned and ran for the back door. Ben held it open. Huntley and Wendell waited outside. Sheila ran out and the door closed behind her. At the bottom of the stairs, she glanced back. Ben had stayed inside.

"Into the woods," Sheila said, leading the way into dark shadows beneath the pines. Under shelter of the trees, they moved slowly along, now in sight of the broken window, now the front door. Glen and Marla stood on the porch. Keys jingled, the door opened. They ran inside. Voices shouted.

"Run for the fence!" Sheila said.

They scrambled out of the woods and ran across short, rugged grasses, yellow in the moonlight. As she ran, Sheila watched for a signal she hoped would be there.

Barbed wire gleamed silver in front of them. Beyond that, a dark void. Where was Katie? Rusty?

Suddenly the air exploded with a deafening sound. Unmistakable. A gunshot. And it came from behind them. *Ben!* Sheila stumbled, half turned.

"Keep going!" Wendell said.

As the noise slowly died, the air filled with another sound. Barking. At the same moment a light flashed. On and off. On and off. The signal.

Katie and Rusty held the bottom strand of wire up. Huntley scrambled under on his stomach. Sheila waited for Wendell, but he refused to go.

"You first," he insisted.

Before she could object, the air exploded again. Another gunshot split the air. "Stop where you are!" Glen shouted.

Sheila threw herself to the ground and wriggled forward like a snake, careful to avoid the sharp barbs.

"This isn't so easy for an old guy like me," Wendell whispered. He creaked down to his hands and knees, and Sheila helped lift the wire a little higher as he crept beneath it. Rebel barked, excited to see his owner.

"Sit, Rebel!" Wendell commanded and the dog was quiet.

Four horses stood waiting, snorting and restless with all the excitement. "You did it!" Sheila said.

"Simple," Rusty said.

"No problem," Katie replied.

Sheila led Wendell to Rusty's horse. "Can you ride?"

"Are you kiddin'? Been ridin' since before I could walk! There's not a horse I can't handle." He grabbed the saddle horn. "Might just need a boost up though," he admitted.

While Sheila helped Wendell, Huntley boosted Katie onto the other quarter horse. He then swung up into Ingot's saddle and Sheila boosted Rusty up behind him. Silver started moving before she was quite in the saddle.

"Get back here you rotten little kids!" Above their heads, a third shot rang out.

Fear in her belly, fear at her back, Sheila wanted to coax Silver into a full gallop. But Katie wasn't ready for that, and even with a few streaks of light hanging over the horizon to the east, the night was still too dark to risk a gallop. So Sheila held Silver to a slow canter and stayed close beside Katie and the other two horses that moved like phantoms up the hill.

Over the muted thud of hoofbeats on grass, Sheila heard a sound that made her want to kick Silver's sides until he put his head down and ran with the speed of light. The honk of a horn, the roar of an engine. She glanced over her shoulder. A bright glow lit the darkness below. Must be the SUV. Voices rose into the air, a man's and a woman's. Katie made a gasping sound, leaned low over her horse's neck and pulled ahead of Sheila.

Silver lengthened his stride, kept pace with Katie's horse. *Hang on, Katie!*

The SUV couldn't get through the fence. Could it? Could it? Wire cutters. All it took was a pair of wire cutters.

The engine noise increased; lights danced on high branches of the pines. Huntley and Wendell reached the trees, disappeared around a bend. Katie and Sheila followed close behind. Around the bend, out of sight. But not for long.

Lights moved toward them, in front of them. Two bright headlights bumping up and down over the grassland. What?

"Quick! Into the trees!" Sheila cried. She led the way into the shelter of tall pines. They stopped and waited. The lights kept coming. The vehicle stopped. The Couttses' SUV, coming from the opposite direction, also stopped. It wheeled around and raced back toward the development. But the second vehicle didn't follow. The lights went out.

Sheila could see it more clearly now. It was a small black Jeep. No roof. Two people in it. "Dad? You there?" a voice called. It was Ryan!

No one moved. No one breathed. Even the horses were silent.

Was Ryan in on this too? Both Ben and Ryan?

Then another voice. "We saw you go into the trees. It's safe now, come on out."

"Mom!" Huntley cried and led his horse out of the woods.

"What now?" Sheila whispered. *Were they all in this together?*

"It's over," Katie told her. "It's okay. I finally figured it out."

They dismounted and walked the horses over to join the others.

"Thank heaven you're all right!" Adele slipped her arm around Huntley. "Ryan said you'd be out here when we discovered you missing."

Sheila glanced nervously at Ryan. She still couldn't believe Ben was the guilty one.

"Have you seen my father?" Ryan asked. "I think he's out here somewhere."

"He's down by the portable," Huntley said, "or inside it. He helped us escape."

"Well, that's one good thing he's done. What happened?"

Sheila and Huntley, with a few words from Wendell, explained what had happened.

"I heard a shot," Sheila said, "after Glen got back."

"The rest of you stay here," Ryan said. "I'm going to find him." He hopped in his Jeep and raced down the hill.

That was the hardest part, waiting and wondering. *Was Ben all right? Had he been shot? Where were the Couttses?*

The sky grew lighter and color returned to the earth, dark green pines, light brown grass. At last Ryan's Jeep bounded back up the hillside and stopped. Ben sat in the passenger seat, slumped forward, clutching his right arm.

"I found him outside the portable," Ryan said. "He tried to make the Couttses follow him, but took a shot in the arm instead."

"Where are the Couttses?" Sheila asked nervously.

"They took off. I don't expect they'll stop until they get home to Calgary."

Ben looked at Sheila. "Ryan wants to take me to Emergency," he said, "but I had to see for myself that you're all okay. Anyway, I figure I deserve whatever happens to me, after what I did."

"Why did you do it, Ben?" Sheila asked.

"Desperation. I figure if your dad and Adele make all this land a wildlife preserve, I'm out of a job. Not just a job, but my home too. I won't have my farrier work to fall back on either, with my elbow getting worse all the time. And here's Ryan needing more and more money for tuition. Thinking about it all made me crazy! Then along comes Marla Coutts and offers me a fantastic job, more money than I ever made in my life! Enough to buy my own house and pay for Ryan's education too. I only had to do a couple of little things to help them get the land for themselves."

"Like shoot the night watchman?" Katie asked.

Ben shook his head. "I just grazed the guy. If he hadn't moved his arm at the last second, the shot would have whizzed past him and hit the window of the portable, like it was meant to."

Sheila knew this was true. Ben never missed his target. "But you set my dad up! How could you do that?"

"I'm so sorry! It's like I lost my mind, couldn't think straight. But I never would have let him go to prison, please believe me. I figured he'd get off easy. No one around here would believe Chris Walton could be involved in anything like that. He's too honest."

"We thought it was Ryan," Sheila admitted. "He's been acting so weird."

They all turned to Ryan.

"I knew something was wrong," Ryan explained. "Dad hasn't been himself since I got here this summer. He's been nervous and jittery, and he kept talking about how he would be out of a job after all these years. So when I heard about the shooting and remembered Dad had been out that night and a rifle was missing, I got suspicious."

"But what about the white feather and the black cowboy hat? Katie saw them in *your* room!" As soon as the words escaped her mouth, Sheila knew she was in trouble.

But Ryan grinned. "I thought that's what you two were up to," he said. "When I found the hat and feather in Dad's room, I knew my suspicions were correct, so I hid them in my room, hoping that would slow him down. I knew he really didn't want to hurt anyone, and I figured he would come to his senses and confess."

"But he went out there tonight."

"Yes. He phoned from town and I told him what you girls told me, that your dad was home and Wendell was watching the development. I had planned on following him and confronting him. I hoped he would turn himself in. But I guess I fell asleep, or he never returned to the cottage, so I didn't realize he parked by the barn and took off in Chris's truck. I finally knew something was up when I found the hat and feather missing. Don't know when he took them, but there you go. He's been pretty sneaky lately."

Ben winced.

"So I hopped in my Jeep to follow. That's when Adele came running out of the house saying you kids were missing. It didn't take much to figure out where you went, especially after she told me Chris was still in police custody."

"And we thought we were being so smart!" Rusty said.

"We are!" Katie insisted. "We proved Sheila's dad is innocent, and we have enough evidence to keep the Couttses out of the way for a long time."

23

*T*he last morning.

Sheila's eyes weren't even open yet, but the words zipped through her head, clear and unavoidable. *The last morning.*

Dad was home, Ben had agreed to testify against the Couttses, and Katie had proudly shared her evidence and notes with the RCMP.

The other good news was that both the Triple W and Cottonwood Creek ranches would be preserved as part of a wildlife corridor that included rangeland along the eastern flank of the Rocky Mountains in southern Alberta. At least in this little corner of the world, grizzly habitat and trumpeter swan wetlands would be safe.

All good.

Except that she had to leave. Today. Gram and GJ would come pick them up, and Sheila would ride out of her father's life again. Maybe for two years, maybe longer. Who knew?

He had Huntley and Adele so close by, why would he bother flying all the way to Victoria just to see her? Sheila groaned. Hadn't meant to, but it slipped out anyway. She held her breath and hoped Katie hadn't heard. But Katie was snoring softly, sound asleep. Good. Sheila rolled out of bed, dressed and tiptoed from the room.

Softly she padded down the stairs and was putting on her shoes when the hall floor creaked. "Sheila, I was hoping you'd get up early so we could go for a ride together!"

She smiled up at her dad. "I'd like that."

Together they galloped across the grasslands, up and over rolling hillocks. Sheila tried to shake her worries free, but for once they stayed with her as she rode.

Later they reined their horses in and walked them side by side. "You okay, Sheila?"

She shrugged. "Fine."

"I hope you realize how grateful I am for all you did."

"It wasn't just me. It was all of us—Huntley too.

And Katie figured it out. She's good at stuff like that."

"Did she figure out why Ben left that rifle under the truck seat?"

"She says Ryan must have come in the back door soon after Ben walked in the front on the *night in question*, so Ben didn't have a chance to put the rifle away. That's what got her confused. She thought Ryan was trying to sneak in to put the rifle back.

"Anyway, Katie figures Ben hid it somewhere in a hurry, maybe under the couch, then pretended to have been sleeping there. He had a busy schedule all the next day, and you were sleeping in the office, so the first chance he got to return it was early the following morning, when you were in the shower. Remember? Everyone else was asleep, except me, and I thought I heard someone in the living room. He must have got scared and run outside with the gun after I went into the kitchen. When you came downstairs, you caught a glimpse of someone wearing blue out near your truck. It wasn't me."

"That's right! He must have hidden it there and never got the chance to put it away with so much going on. I still can't believe Ben would do such a thing."

After a moment of silence he added, "It's a good

thing you kids were here. But, Sheila, it really scares me to think what might have happened out there. Promise me you won't do anything like that again?"

"Dad..." What could she say? How could she make a promise like that when she had a friend like Katie? Luckily her dad changed the subject.

"Your mother will go crazy when I tell her."

"Then maybe you shouldn't tell her."

"I need to, Sheila. It wouldn't be right to keep secrets from your mother. She'd never forgive me if something were to happen to you. I'm going to phone her this morning."

Sheila felt ill. Mom would be furious and probably insist that Sheila come right home. Hadn't Sheila promised not to get involved in anything dangerous while she was away?

"Besides, I want to ask her something. If it's all right with you, of course."

"What?"

"I was hoping you might consider staying here, with me, for the rest of the summer."

"Really? You really want me to?"

"Of course. We haven't had much time to visit yet."

"No. Yes! Dad, I'd love to stay! I can't believe it! What about Huntley?"

"Huntley? He's a great kid, but he's not you. You're my daughter, Sheila, and I love you." Her dad grinned and tapped Pita's flanks. "Last one back has to wash all the breakfast dishes!" he called over his shoulder.

"Hey! No fair!" Sheila shouted. She tapped Silver and took off after her father.

No place to live

Some strange beings move into your neighborhood. They destroy your home so you and your family have nowhere to live. They tear down all the grocery stores so you can't find any food. What will you do? Where will you go?

Such a scary incident is not likely to happen to you, but it does happen to wildlife all over the world when human development encroaches on wilderness areas. Luckily, many people are working to save both plants and animals by conserving important habitat.

Preserving wildlife habitat

Canada is a huge country with a small population. This is good news for wildlife because we still have more wild spaces than many other countries do. Rugged coastlines, dense rain forests, high mountain ranges, deep river valleys and rolling grasslands support an amazing variety of wildlife. However, the human population keeps growing, especially in the south. More than 90 percent of Canada's population lives in only

10 percent of our country, closest to the US border. More people means more houses, more buildings, more roads and more parking lots, so it's not surprising that 70 percent of Canada's wildlife species at risk also occupies this region along our southern border.

Wetlands are filled in, forests are cut down, grasslands are converted to agricultural use. As a result, many of Canada's plant and animal species are in danger of losing their habitat. When human development encroaches on wilderness areas, species can become threatened because they don't have enough space to live, find food and reproduce.

An organization that is working hard to save important habitat lands is the Nature Conservancy of Canada. NCC is a national organization that is "dedicated to preserving ecologically significant areas" in every part of the country. When an important type of habitat is threatened, NCC moves in to help. Of course, no one can save every piece of wilderness land, so NCC concentrates on the most ecologically significant areas. To decide which areas are most important, NCC relies on conservation science.

When an ecologically diverse area has been identified by scientists, NCC works with local people and environmental groups to help preserve this important habitat. One way it does this is by helping property owners to remain on their land and preserve it as a conservation easement.

A conservation easement means that the owner agrees to certain restrictions on the land, such as never subdividing it and not allowing the trees to be cut down or new construction to be built. In some cases, ranchers can also sell their land to NCC and then lease back a portion of it. Conservation easements allow ranching families to remain on their land and continue to work it. At the same time they help preserve the area for native plants and animals.

One of NCC's biggest successes is the Waterton Lake Front Project in southwestern Alberta. Land adjacent to Waterton Lakes National Park has been preserved for indigenous species that include grizzly bears and trumpeter swans. NCC worked with the W. Garfield Weston Foundation to create a large conservation easement and, at the same time, help landowners preserve their land.

Nature Conservancy Canada also works closely with a larger organization, the Nature Conservancy. The Nature Conservancy has projects all over the United States, North America and the world. Like NCC, one way the Nature Conservancy works to preserve habitat is by conservation easements.

Learn more about Nature Conservancy Canada and find out what projects are happening near your home by checking out its website at www.natureconservancy.ca.

You can find information on the Nature Conservancy and its projects around North America and the world at www.nature.org.

More about grizzlies

Grizzly bears are large animals that require a huge range for each individual. Depending upon the amount of food available, a female grizzly may have a range of up to 1000 square kilometers. A grizzly's range is easily disturbed by development. On the eastern slopes of the Rocky Mountains, human pressures and habitat loss threaten the bears' existence. But grizzlies still survive in Banff National Park and areas surrounding the park in Alberta.

A ranch like the one in *Alberta Alibi* could be part of a grizzly's range. The Eastern Slope Grizzly Bear Project (ESGBP) is studying grizzlies on the eastern slopes of the Rockies so people can learn the best way to manage and conserve these magnificent animals.

For more information on the ESGBP and on grizzly bears, go to the website at www.canadianrockies.net/Grizzly.

Trumpeter swans

Trumpeters are the largest species of swan. They were once abundant in North America, but their numbers dwindled when they were shot for their feathers and their meat. They are now a protected species.

Trumpeter swans winter in wet areas of British Columbia, Washington and northern Oregon. Most migrate in spring to nest in places such as Alaska, Minnesota, Wisconsin, Alberta and the Yukon. Safe wetlands, such as "Swan Pond" in *Alberta Alibi*, help trumpeter swans find sufficient food and reproduce. The good news is that conservation projects to help preserve trumpeter swan habitat are increasing their numbers from near extinction.

For more information on trumpeter swans, go to www.trumpeterswansociety.org/.

Dayle Campbell Gaetz is the author of two other thrilling mysteries featuring her trio of determined detectives: *Mystery From History,* an OLA Silver Birch nominee, and *Barkerville Gold.* Dayle lives in Campbell River, British Columbia.